MW01532230

TORN

A Novel by Antonio Torres

Outskirts Press, Inc.
Denver, Colorado

This is a work of fiction. The events and characters described herein are imaginary and are not intended to refer to specific places or living persons. The opinions expressed in this manuscript are solely the opinions of the author and do not represent the opinions or thoughts of the publisher.

Torn
All Rights Reserved.
Copyright © 2008 Antonio Torres
V3.0

This book may not be reproduced, transmitted, or stored in whole or in part by any means, including graphic, electronic, or mechanical without the express written consent of the publisher except in the case of brief quotations embodied in critical articles and reviews.

Outskirts Press, Inc.
http://www.outskirtspress.com

ISBN: 978-1-4327-2864-9

Outskirts Press and the "OP" logo are trademarks belonging to Outskirts Press, Inc.

PRINTED IN THE UNITED STATES OF AMERICA

Acknowledgements

I would like to thank my heavenly father, the Lord Jesus Christ for looking over my family and keeping them free from harm.

I'd like to thank my mom, Sonia Rodriguez without her none of this would have been possible and my stepdad Jose Rodriguez. To my beautiful sisters Cookie, Lilly, Debbie, and Barbie. To Phillip Bracco Thanks for giving me a chance.

To my nephew Jason Gomez – stick with me kid, I'll be your dad if you need me.

Janet Rizzi, Christina Rodriguez, Big Vin, and little Vin. I'm blessed to have a second family like you. To Anthony Rodriguez and John Ramirez Thank you for your help.

John of J.P's Seafood Restaurant – thank you for the support, the clams, the sangria, and for giving my sister an incredible wedding party.

To Big Chris, Dreamboy, Rob Desire, and Nastee boy for your support.

Thank you Miles Mahoney your mentorship and support has been a blessing.

Jesus Maymi -thank you for your blessings, prayers, and the "Writer's Digest".

Patrick Darge, David Trasoras, Maria Tirado, Richard Murillo, Brenda Santiago, Elizer Tejada, Robert Pantori, Raymond Rosado, and John Victor Pena.

To Jimmy McGerald for teaching me a skill I will treasure for the rest of my life.

Antoine "Inch" Thomas - for giving me the inspiration and guidance to carry out this project. To Zelma, my editor, for helping me put this thing together.

To Melissa Bonilla I love you baby, lets make it happen.

A very special thanks to my beautiful angel - my sister Barbie. May you be as happy as you deserve to be with your new husband. Jimmy Z, take care of my angel.

Torn

I t was past midnight in the parking lot of the Carlton Hotel and Ray was leaning on the hood of his Lexus GS 400, both elbows on the hood, bent at the waist. His partner, Frankie, was sitting in the passenger's seat with a nine millimeter pistol on his lap. Frankie, sticking his head out the window, called out to Ray.

"Yo, what time is he supposed to be here?"

"I don't know—midnight maybe?" said Ray.

"Well you know it's 12:30 right?

"Relax bro, he'll be here alright? Damn."

A figure crept up behind the car stealthily. It then stood up and opened its arms.

"Yo Ray!" shouted the figure.

Ray moved away from the hood and looked towards the back of the car, where the voice had originated.

"Hey, what's up bro? I've been waiting since midnight, what happened?"

"Oh, you know —just got caught up at the airport. You know, since

9-11 all the security has been off the hook. Ray, this is my brother-in-law Chino."

"What's up Chino." said Ray.

Chino nodded, confirming his identity.

"Let me get that stuff for you bro." said Ray, his attention back on his friend.

Ray walked towards the back of the car and leaned in through the open door, pulling out "that" bag—the one that guy had come for. A single drop of sweat slid down Ray's face. He knew it wouldn't go down that easy. Without warning, Ray dug into his pocket and pulled out a chrome 9 millimeter. In a stroke of bad luck, the 9 millimeter got stuck in Ray's oversized jersey, giving the guy enough time to react and wrench the pistol out of his hand. At the same time, Chino had managed to grab Frank's neck into a headlock, in an attempt to wrestle the gun out off of him. With the butt of Ray's own gun, the guy smacked the right side of Ray's head. The blow rocked Ray badly, and brought him to his knees. At that moment, Chino managed to wrestle the 9 millimeter off of Frankie, turning his own gun against Frankie's temple. Right before Ray could regain his composure, he was sent crashing to the floor with another blow against his head. A wide split appeared on the left side of his forehead.

The guys, still unnamed, called out to Chino.

"Chino are you alright?"

"Yeah man, you?"

"Yeah man. I'm good. I can't believe this motherfucker man! He was going to kill me, why?" he shouted.

He turned around in a frenzy and started screaming.

"You piece of shit! You fuckin' cocksucker? Why? Why you fuck?"

Ray in silence offered no response.

"Give me the key to the motherfuckin' room, now! You fuckin' scumbag!"

Ray gave him the bloodied key.

"Now get up and get in the fuckin' room you worm!"

He grabbed Ray by the back of his jersey and dragged him towards the door of the room, while simultaneously "pistol whipping" him on the back of his head. Ray opened the door and Chino forced Frankie inside.

"Take off your clothes!" Chino yelled in his Spanish accent.

Frankie stripped completely.

"Now get over there in that corner, and get on your knees!"

Frankie immediately obeyed. However, Ray remained at the foot of the door on his hands and knees.

"Get up!" said the guy.

Ray began to push himself up, but just as he was about to get on his feet the guy took a step back and plunged his foot square across Ray's back, sending him crashing onto the hotel room floor. Frankie stayed in the corner, shaking like a leaf.

"Ray! Get on your knees now!"

Ray lay there in silence without moving. The guy, infuriated, ran up, put the pistol against Ray's cheekbone, and slowly and deliberately said, *"Get on your fuckin' knees before I blast your fuckin' ass, motherfucker!"*

Ray complied and finally knelt in front of the guy. The guy put a single finger under Ray's chin and positioned his face so that he could look directly into Ray's eyes.

"Ray, bro, you were going to kill me? Over money bro? All of the things we've shared, all the times we've had, and all the money we've made? Yet, you were going to kill me over $30,000 bro?"

Crrraaaack! He delivered yet another blow against Ray's already injured forehead. Infuriated, the guy continued to bashing away at the wound on Ray's head. The more he bashed, the more blood gushed out of the wound. Ray started to make a slight swerving movement, as if he was on the verge of passing out. In an effort to avoid any more pain Ray swung his arm across the gun as it was coming down for another blow.

"BAM!"

The gun went off and Ray crumbled over like a bag of rocks. He clutched his chest and looked up at the guy as he stood over him.

"Let me go to the hospital, please!" Ray pleaded.

The guy stood there in silence, shocked over what had just happened. Chino looked over at Frankie kneeling in the corner and yelled at him.

"Don't you fucking move from there!"

"Please., please, bro let me go to the hospital. I won't say anything to anybody. Please bro, I swear on my life bro. Come on you know my wife bro, and I would never want to put her life in jeopardy. Let me go get this taken care of please!" pleaded Ray.

The guy took three steps back away from Ray and said,

"Ray, you told me you had money, and despite that it's been over seven months that I've been waiting. I never threatened or harassed you for it. As a matter of fact, you called me to come and meet you—

that you had my money already. You called me bro. Why would you want to kill me Ray?

The silence was deafening.

"I'm leaving Ray. When I leave, your friend can take you to the hospital.

1500 Miles North

Knock knock knock - the door opened. He walked in and looked to the left, down the long corridor that lead to the living room, kitchen, bathroom and the two bedrooms. It was quiet, a little too quiet. He had been here before on some of the quietest days and never had it been this quiet. He stood there, staring down the corridor to his left, waiting for some sort of justification as to why it was so quiet. Standing there, he slowly threw his right hand behind him—catching the door and slowly shutting it. He broke his stare away from the corridor and looked to his right, where the third bedroom door was wide open. He entered the bedroom.

"Close the door" she said.

He obediently closed the door and looked at her, staying close to the door. It was plain to see that something was wrong. It just wasn't the norm. She didn't look happy to see him. She wasn't bubbling over with excitement like she usually was.

"What"? he asked .

She stood quiet, almost as if she was making a mental count. 30 seconds later she came to life and asked

"Tony, do you love me"?

"Baby, of course I love you, you know that, why on earth would even"

Without warning the door swung open and a second woman entered the room.

"How the fuck could you do this to me Tony!? Why the fuck Tony? Why? Haven't I been good to you?!

Tears fell from the second woman's eyes and stained her beautiful pale cheeks with dark eyeliner. Tony glanced to his left and saw the first woman, just sitting there - the mastermind of this whole fiasco, eyes swelled, tears trickling down her face and staining her rose colored cheeks with mascara. His heart was crushed.

"Tony, how could you do this to me? How can you betray my love like that? I work all fucking day, hard Tony, 12 hours a day, and this is what you do while I'm at work?!" yelled the first woman.

She was clearly crying her heart out. Standing by the door, were five other women - sisters and mothers of the two girls involved. These were the women to whom he had promised never to hurt either of the girls. They stood there expecting an explanation that he could not give. From the right came screams and tears, from the left came silence and tears, and in his heart arose a bone-crushing pain for fear of losing either one of these beautiful women. He would never be able to express to them how much he loved them.

Just watching their agony made him wish he were dying in a burning car, rather than seeing them suffer this way. He had promised to make them happy. At the moment, however, he just stood there in silence, his heart hammering so loud, he could've sworn it was audible. It hurt so much, he couldn't even speak.

"What are you going to do now, huh? Is it going to be me or her? Choose now Tony, now!"

He looked at the second girl standing near the door, then to the girl sitting on the bed, just sobbing her little broken heart out. Based on past experiences, this should have been an easy choice to make, right? All he had to do was look at them, weigh the options, see

6

which one he loved more, and choose. Tony, however, was born without the chromosome that would allow him to be cold and unsympathetic. He knew that choosing one would make the other one hurt even more, and yes, he tried to weigh the options and compare them but they were both equal to him.

Both were extremely gorgeous in their own respective ways, both loving, great families, incredible human beings, and amazing in bed. Again the screams came from the door.

"Do you love her Tony? Tell me now!"

Tony asked himself, "Why is it that when these situations present themselves, the only question that seems to be of any importance to them is *"Do you love her?"* I don't get it."

He felt as if he was in the middle of a tornado.

At the moment, he decided that the best thing for him to do was to put his arms around his back, grab his wrist tightly to avoid any physical reactions, and clench his teeth in preparation for the slap that he knew would eventually come. He lowered his head in shame and thought to himself, *"My God, I have to make a choice right here and now. Please help me to do this right."*

He waited, and waited, but nothing came. Perhaps God wanted him to stew in his own juices for awhile. Tony looked to his left, straight into those beautiful brown eyes that he loved so much, and then to his right, straight into those gorgeous moist eyes that he adored so immensely. He definitely couldn't choose. He looked past the one on his right, only to discover that the front door to the house was slightly open.

"I don't believe you Tony!"

The second girl threw her hands up in the air, and as she turned, she left enough room for him to beeline right past her and through the door. He ran downstairs, jumped into his car, and pulled out of there like a bat out of hell.

24 Months Earlier

Tony pushed open the rear exit doors to *Club Mystique* to grab a smoke. He leaned up against the wall, through his foot up, and gazed up at the sky while inhaling deep puffs of his cigarette. As he started to take another drag, he heard the roaring engine of an all too familiar sound.

Right away he sounded off, *"911 Carrera, twin turbo, am I right?" He ran around to the front of the club and smiled.*

"Damn I'm good."

A canary yellow Porsche 911 pulled in. He heard the distinguished sounds of the roaring engine as it pulled into a parking space. Tony took another drag and held it in while he admired the car. The engine shut off and the door swung open to reveal a tall, slender, good looking gentleman with dashing looks and clad with top of the line duds. Prada shoes, Versace shirt, and Armani pants were just some of the things he noticed. It was evident that he was making a substantial amount of money. He glanced at Tony, saw him puffing on a smoke, and acknowledged him by nodding. Tony nodded back. He watched the gentleman enter the club and ran around toward the back of the building. He turned out the cigarette and went back inside.

The music was thumping to the heavy bass beats of the Ibiza soundtracks. Tony took a peek from behind the velvet curtains, only to see an overwhelming 500 women or so, screaming and dancing in anticipation of the award-winning all male revenue. He closed the curtains and went into a nearby dressing room.

"Okay fellas, I'm first. Nastee boy—you're second, Rob Desire— you're third, Flava—you're fourth, and Chris Dream boy—you're last."

He headed towards Chris, gave him a quick high five, and whispered into his ear.

"Gotta save my best for last."

They looked at each for a moment and smiled. Chris Dream boy was Tony's number one guy. They loved each other like brothers—with Chris looking out for Tony like a bodyguard would. At 6' 1" and 230 lbs., he was a huge and commanding presence to say the least.

One night, Tony had hired another guy onto the team, for a one-night show at a place called "Sidestreets" in the Bronx. That night, things got a little hairy. Over 500 women showed up at a place with a 250 person capacity. Tony, being the problem solver that he was, decided to divide the show into two back-to-back shows, splitting the amount of women in half. They were all changing in the bathroom when he walked in and told the guys the situation.

"Guys, I've got good news and bad news. What do you want first?"

"What's the good news?" asked Nastee boy.

"Well, the good news is that instead of 300 women showing up, we have the 300 plus 200 and change waiting to get in—and we haven't even started."

The guys all screamed *"Yeah baby"*, and slapped each other high-fives, knowing this would be a financial success for everyone on the team.

"So what could the bad news be?" asked Rob Desire.

"Well, the bad news is we're going to have to do two shows back-to-back, each for 250 women."

"So what?" said Rob.

"Well the thing is I may not be able to pay for the second show."

"I see no problem with that." said Big Chris.

"Yeah bro, come on bro, we'll just do what we came to do." said Nastee boy.

"The owner doesn't want to pay me anymore money, so what I'll do is I'll give you my pay, fuck it"

"Na, na, na, I ain't gonna let you do that bro. Stop the bullshit." said Chris.

"Yeah Tony, don't worry about that shit. We'll do both shows. Keep your money." said Rob.

"Na, na. fuck that shit. If I'm gonna do the show—I'm getting paid twice. I come from Chippendales." said the new guy.

All the guys looked at Tony, waiting for his reaction. They knew what he was capable of, but he wasn't going to get hot-headed before a show of this caliber. So, he decided that he would try an be a gentleman about the whole situation. He turned to the new guy and said,

"Ok, check this out my man. If you want to leave now, I'll give you gas money so that you don't feel like I've wasted your time. Either that, or you can do the show for regular pay and all the tips the five hundred women will be giving you."

The kid stepped up to Tony and said, *"Na, I'm getting paid double for the show or full pay for coming down here and wasting my time, or there's gonna be some shit poppin' off in here!"*

Tony placed his hands on his waist, looked down, and shook his head in disbelief, when suddenly; he was slammed against the wall. All Tony could see for a moment was Chris' huge back in front of him as he thrust his foot into the new guy's sternum.

As the new guy fell backwards, Rob Desire stepped behind him and prevented his head from smashing into the white porcelain urinal by grabbing it into a lock.

Chris stepped up to the guy, eye to eye, while Rob held him up.

"We're a family bro" said Chris, " and that's my little brother there. So if there's gonna be some shit poppin off in here—then you best pop it with me. So what's up Mr. Chippendale?"

Before the new guy could get a word out, he was out cold. Big Chris had swung a 60 mph elbow right at his cheekbone, cracking open a fresh wound. Chris looked back at Tony and said,

"Sorry I pushed you so hard."

He extended his arm to pick Tony up. All the guys looked at him and said, *"Ready to Rock and Roll?"*

"Let's go," replied Tony.

From that moment on, Tony knew he had inherited Chris as a bodyguard.

Tony snapped back to reality when, back in Club Mystique, the MC began his rant.

"Ladies are you ready to see some 100% grade A, all American beef?"

Blaring screams came from all over the crowd of drunk, horny women. The screams were deafening.

"How many of you ladies like hot Latin men?"

The screams grew louder and louder.

"Then ladies, without any further delay, I introduce to you, your Latin lover Antonio—known as Zorro!!!"

The screams became so loud that Tony was hardly able to hear his opening music. The guitar strings from his into music started playing. With each guitar string pulled, Tony took a step closer to the stage. When he finally appeared on stage, the women roared in approval. Something about the combination of hundreds of women, music, alcohol, and putting them all in a room with half-naked men was exciting to him. He drew his sword and started emulating the Zorro character by swinging the sword in a "Z". Tony deliberately unbuttoned his shirt slowly. The women were losing their minds. Through the corner of his eye, Tony noticed someone approaching him.

He tried to remain focused, when suddenly; he felt a tug on his shirt. A girl from the audience completely ripped off Tony's shirt in one swift motion.

The crowd roared in approval of what this intoxicating beauty had just done.

He smiled, gave the girl a kiss, and signaled security to come haul her off stage. He ended up doing a thirty-minute performance, throughout which women spent their time screaming. He ran back-stage drenched in sweat. The guys looked at him, and he gave them a thumbs-up.

"Yeah guys. They're fine and there's a lot of money out there, so go get it guys!"

Two hours later, Tony was sitting at the bar. He looked across the dance floor to see Nastee grinding away on the dance floor, sandwiched by a bevy of beauties. Rob Desire was on the other side, tongue deep in some girl's esophagus. Flava had six girls surrounding him, tearing away at him. To Tony's right, Chris Dream boy sat at a table with two beautiful blondes fondling each other while sitting on his lap.

This life he lived—*"Gotta love it"*, he thought. He restrained himself, however, until he was finished doing business. He signaled

Torn

the guys over to the bar and handed them each an envelope with their day's pay. Some left and some stayed—it was always like that. Afterwards, he called the bartender and ordered a drink.

"Mojito please."

"Sure Tony, coming right up", replied the bartender.

Tony looked across the bar and noticed the flamboyant Versace shirt he had seen earlier in the parking lot. It was Mr. 911, the owner of his dream car. As the bartender arrived with his drink, Tony signaled the bartender over to him and asked,

"Jimmy, who's the guy at the end of the bar? *You know this is a "ladies only" event tonight. What's he doing here?"*

"I don't know Tony. I think he's with the owner. I think he's an investor looking to buy the club."

Tony suddenly felt a pat on his back. The owner of the club, Artie, swung a friendly arm over Tony's shoulder and sat down next to him.

"Tony my man, another successful one my friend."

Tony held his drink up and toasted with Artie.

"To many more, Artie."

"Yeah to many more. I just wish you would buy this damn place off me already Tony. I'm getting old."

"Artie my friend, you want too much money baby. When are you gonna come down on the price for me?"

"I don't think I have to Tony. See that guy over there at the end of the bar?"

13

Artie signaled over the Versace shirt guy.

"Yeah."

"Well, he's here to check out the place, and hopefully, to make me a full price offer."

The guy approached the two men.

"Hey George!"

Artie greeted the Versace shirt guy, George, with a formal hug. They nodded and shook hands.

"Now George, remember that if you want to buy this place, you have to take it with Tony included. That's the way the deal will go if we do it."

"Sure, sure that wouldn't be a problem."

"Guys excuse me", Artie excused himself after being suddenly called over by an employee.

After they were alone, Tony turned to George.

"So George, looking to buy the place, huh?"

"Well, yeah. Is this your show? I mean, did you put all of this together by yourself?"

"Yup, it was all me. Those were my guys and my girls—I have 2,500 women only mailing list."

"So with all this success in what you do, why haven't you bought the club?"

"Well I really can't afford what Artie's asking for."

Torn

George nodded in understanding.

"Let me ask you a question. If you had more money than he was asking for, Would you buy this club or would you buy another club?"

"I think I would buy this one. I'm pretty stable here. The word is out that the hottest male revenue is held here on the last Friday of each month. "It's established and hell, why mess with a well oiled running machine?"

"I think we'd get along well if I bought this place. I like your way of thinking. Do you have a business card?"

"Yeah, here."

Tony handed George a business card and asked,

"So, you think you're gonna buy it?"

"Don't know Tony, but I'll give you a call tomorrow."

He shook Tony's hand, got up, and left. Tony took a sip of his Mojito and wondered for a moment about why George might want to call him. Artie finally returned.

"Where's George?"

"He left. He said he'll call you tomorrow."

"Oh, ok."

Artie sat down on a stool and glanced around the club.

"Hey Tony, do you feel that?" Artie asked.

'No, feel what?"

15

"Bro, that girl is burning a hole in your back. She's been checking you out for some time, both her and her girlfriend."

Tony turned around to see two goddesses smiling with Artie. He shook his head as Artie left the bar.

"That a boy Tony. Go gettem."

"Dirty job but somebody's got to do it," replied Tony.

Later that night...

Moans and groans filled the air.

"Oh Tony, baby!"

"Yeah girl, come on. Talk to me baby."

Her name was Jessie. She was 5' 7" tall and 150 lbs. spread equally all over her body. She was a fitness competitor, tight, strong, and insane flexibility. As Tony kissed her navel, she moaned and guided his head with her hand to look at her.

When he did she said,

"Take me into your mouth baby."

She sat at the edge of her bed and spread her legs wide open to reveal her ripe tender fruit overflowing with juices that glistened with the candlelight flicker. She lifted her leg up straight towards the ceiling and held it there as she asked Tony to indulge in her moist flower. He knelt down, and placed his right hand underneath her left hamstring assisting her as she held her leg up. With the tip of his tongue, he gently and delicately licked her moistened folds. Her wet pussy made an inhaling sound as he grazed his tongue over it. Tony went up toward her clit and flickered his tongue over it, barely touching it, but enough for her to feel the light graze of his flicker.

Torn

He stood on that beautiful little bean and flickered relentlessly as she moaned for him not to stop.

"Aieee take me Tony. Please take me now."

He came up and looked at her. She had a tear of pleasure in her eye.

"Si papi, yeah fuck me baby, ahora papi."

Tony stood up, grabbed his hard stiff pipe, stroked it twice, smiled, and went back down to the slurp of lava spilling down the inside of her thighs. He stood up, held both legs open, and started penetrating her vulva with his tongue. The sound of his tongue gliding in and out of her vulva was making her increasingly hornier and louder.

"Oh please Tony—do it now papi—fuck me!"

Tony got up off his knees and grabbed his dick. He guided his throbbing tool toward her throbbing pussy but didn't put it in. He pressed it up against her glimmering wet slit and stroked it in an up and down fashion just over the folds of her pussy, teasing the life out of her. In one swift motion, she deliberately swung up, grabbed his waist, and pulled

Tony into her. His cock plunged right into her soft, heated pussy. Her mission: to envelop his cock and bring herself to the ultimate climax. At the fourth stroke she exploded into a convulsed climax screaming at the top of her lungs.

"Ohh my god, oh my god, oh my god, aaiiiee fuck, fuckk aaii si papi que pinga, oh oh oh oh I'm coming aaaahhhyy!"

Jessie sat there breathing hard and gasping for air. Her breathing then died down a bit before she said,

"Baby I want you to come now."

Jessie and Tony sat up, looked over at the chaise lounge, and smiled

17

at Samantha who sat on the chaise naked—drilling her wet pussy with her fingers while they had been indulging with each other.

Samantha slid down off the chaise, got on her hands and knees and crawled over to them in a cat-like manner. She grabbed both of Tony's knees and pulled herself up a bit. She spread his legs open to reveal his stiff cock just waiting for her. She grabbed his dick with her left hand and began to lick the head while simultaneously massaging his balls with her right hand. She took him so deep into her mouth that his cock felt like it was in an oven. As soon as she started stroking it, he was ready to explode.

"Ahh, I'm coming baby."

She took it out of her mouth and started stroking it furiously, while looking at Tony in the eyes,

"Come on baby, show me that milk. Come on baby, tell me when—come on baby, come in mouth, fuck."

"NOW!" cried Tony.

She took Tony in deep once again as he shook fiercely. She pulled it out again only to have him spurt the rest all over her face and hair. She kept stroking and stroking, blanketing his cock with her mouth until he was dry. She looked at him, smiled, and crawled into the bed. Tony pushed himself back onto his pillow. Both girls raised their heads as he slid his arm under their necks. They nestled themselves comfortably to sleep.

Later that morning…

Bzzzz, bzzzz, bzzzz - a vibrating sound awoke Tony. Barely awake he said,

"Ok, who has the vibrator? It's too early for that shit."

Finally opening his eyes, he noticed that both of the girls were still asleep. His cell phone was vibrating. Tony hastily picked up the phone.

"Hello?"

"Tony?'

"Yeah, who's this?"

"It's me George."

"George who?"

"Me, George, from last night-the club?"

"Oh, oh yeah. Hey, what's up?"

"Did I wake you?"

"Na, na just resting up."

"Babe, tell them to call back later. Come to bed", said Jessie.

"Yeah, you got all day to talk to them", said Samantha.

"Hey Tony, you having a party over there?" George asked excitedly.

"Na, na I just have some close friends come over last night", Tony said modestly.

"Oh. Hey look, the reason I'm calling is because I'd like to make you a business proposition."

"Oh yeah, well talk to me."

"No buddy, not on the phone. The best business is always discussed in person, so why don't you meet me at J.P's Restaurant say 1:00 p.m. We'll have coffee, some grub, and we'll iron out the details of my

19

proposal to see if you're interested, What ya say?"

"Yeah, yeah one o'clock is fine. Ok, later."

"Later."

Tony shut off the phone.

JP's Restaurant

Tony entered the restaurant and is greeted by the host, a good-looking lady in her early 40s. She must have been smokin' hot when she was 20, but time took its toll and seem she was trying hard to stay young.

"Hello, will you be eating alone today?"

"No, I'm waiting for someone."

"Okay, I'll set the table for two.

Tony took his seat at the booth.

"Your waitress will be right with you."

"Thank you", said Tony.

A few moments later, his waitress appeared.

"Hi, my name is Kristina and I'll be your waitress today. Can I start you off with something to drink?"

Tony was immediately taken back by how beautiful this young lady was. She must have been 5' 6", 120 lbs. slim, and model-like. She was incredibly beautiful. Tony looked at her and was thrown into some cosmic place where he became temporarily deaf and dumb.

"Heeeeeelllllooooo? Are you there?"

"Oh, I'm sorry. It's that you look so familiar. You probably get that a lot. Anyway yeah, just bring me a pitcher of sangria with extra fruit."

"Anything to eat?" she asked.

"No, not yet. I'm still waiting for someone, just sangria for now."

"Ok, I'll be back with your sangria."

Looking out the restaurant window on a beautiful, sunny Saturday afternoon—coming over the city island bridge there it was. Like a bumblebee doing a 90 mph, a yellow dot was what Tony saw for 90 seconds. As it approached, it transformed into the beast that he one day vowed to own—a Porsche 911. He watched the yellow beast reverse tightly into a spot. George stepped out from within and strutted into the restaurant. Tony waved so that he was sure to see him.

"Hey, what's up Tony?"

George stuck his hand out and Tony shook it. Tony looked through the window at the car and without breaking the stare he said,

"Hey George, if you don't mind my asking, how much did you pay for your car?"

"Oh not much, why? You like it?'

"Yeah bro, I love that damn car. It's my dream car."

"Oh yeah, well who knows…Maybe your dreams will come true soon enough. Anyway, Tony what I'm here to propose is a partnership. Look I love the club scene and I love what you did at Mystiques the other night. Can you do that anywhere?"

"Yeah, as long as I have ample space." It seemed to Tony that George had the means, he just needed "the know".

"George, are you really going to buy Mystiques?"

"Uhh, I don't know. Artie is in his sixties and I really don't like partnerships with people who are much older than me. They get cranky, unrealistic, and eventually become pain in the asses. See Tony, you're young like me—on fire and hungry to become a success. I can see it in your eyes. I want to partner up with someone like myself so that we can become young millionaires. You see I have a feeling that we're gonna get along great. How old are you?"

"31"

"You see I'm 34. We both love the club scene and damn Tony, two girls? Last night? That's what I'm talking about baby. Can you teach me that shit? That mojo you got?"

Tony thought to himself for a moment. This guy was good looking, green eyes, and appeared to have a decent amount of money, and he was having girl trouble? Something was clearly wrong.

"Mojo?' asked Tony, *"What are you talking about bro? You tellin' me you can't pick up girls?"*

"Well lets just say, I wasn't born with the gift of gab, you on the other hand know how to rap, have a good physique, have all those moves with the ladies bro—all you need is a nice 911 and you'll be straight heh?"

"Yeah, I wish."

"Well look, I've got a friend who sells used Porsches, maybe I'll call him up and se what's the best he can do for me."

'Sounds good."

"So you think you're interested in partnering up?"

"Well George, I'll tell you what—let me think about it and we'll meet

here tomorrow in time for lunch."

"Alright, sounds good bro. By the way, what's your last name?"

"Falcon, why?"

"Couldn't tell if you were Spanish or Italian. Mine is Selbor."

"What's that? I mean nationality?"

"Ah, it doesn't even matter bro, I'll see you tomorrow."

"Ok, later."

George shook hands with Tony and promptly left. Tony gazed out the window as George jumped into his car and took off. He admired the car once more as it disappeared onto the onramp of the highway. He looked down to get the check and noticed a one hundred dollar bill that George left to cover the bill. Nice move, he thought, he hadn't even noticed that shit. Lunch was only twenty-two dollars. He flagged the waitress over and handed her the bill with the check. As she took it and walked away, Tony's eyes followed her all the way back to the cash register. Damn, what wouldn't he give to be waking up next to that girl every morning.

On her way back with the change, Tony met up with the girl halfway there and handed her a thirty-dollar tip.

"Uhh, excuse me sir?"

"Yes."

Tony turned around and looked into her beautiful light brow eyes.

"Sir this tip..."

"What it's not enough?" Tony interrupted.

"No, it's too much."

"Why is it too much? Because somebody mandated that 15% should be your tip, because you don't think you're worth it, or because everyone who you've served up until now hasn't realized the rare quality that you display when you serve, and how extremely beautiful you are? If you ask me a $30 tip is below what you deserve, but I'll be coming here often and, if I give you more, I'll be broke before I retire."

The pretty waitress laughed.

"Thank you. That's a nice thing to say."

"Anytime. Hey, what's your name again?"

"Kristina."

"Well Kristina, once again, you are beautiful."

With that, Tony turned around and left without awaiting a response. Kristina, on the other hand, was left blushing. Kristina, a blonde, light-skinned beauty was a timid twenty-year old girl. She had never dated a customer in her two years working at the diner.

After making her way into the kitchen of the restaurant, she was immediately greeted by all eight of her curious co-workers.

"Well?" asked Kyle.

"Well what?"

"Oh come off it Kristy" Said Sandy.

"Ya'll bitches need to stop" replied Kristina.

"How much did the gay cuties leave you?"

Kristina laughed, *"I don't think they're gay. Fine they are but gay ah - I don't think so.*

Anyway, they're bill was $22 and he gave me a $30 tip."

"$30??" screamed Kyle.

"Bitch, what you giving blowjobs in the parking lot or something?" Mandy asked.

They all laughed and slapped each other high fives.

"Now we know they're gay" said Kyle.

"What makes you say that?" asked Kristina.

"Hello girl, don't you know by now little Kristy, that straight men do not tip like that for starters, secondly they came to meet each other, they dress extremely well, they are good looking, they really didn't look at you, and they ordered fruity sangria. Straight men just don't do that."

"They're gay." all the girls said in unison.

Kristina sighed in disappointment. *"Oh well, gay men do make the best of friends."*

Saturday Night at Mystiques

The door slammed shut as Tony exited the cab. He stood in the parking lot as he lit up his cigarette. He scanned the parking lot, not really knowing what he was looking for, but noticed two very intoxicated, exotic women making out in between a Hummer h3 and a Suburban. They looked up only to see that they seemed to have a voyeur on their hands. One of them signaled him over and said,

"You want in on this?"

Antonio Torres

Tony leaned against the Hummer and took a long drag of his cigarette.

"Just make like I'm not here baby."

"Hmmm, three tongues are better than two."

"Let me soak the both of you first."

They continued their frolicking and tit groping. One of the girls looked back at Tony,

"We love being stared at. It makes us hornier. The thrill of knowing we can get caught, just like you caught us, makes my pussy pulse."

At the same time, she pulled out a pink pocket rocket. With her left hand she scooped up her partner's skirt, and with her right hand, she was readied herself to glide that little pocket rocket into that throbbing wet vulva. At that point, Tony's phone rang and he was taken out of the trance that he was in.

"Fuuuuck!"

"Hello."

"Tony?"

"Yeah, who's this?"

"Its Artie are you coming down tonight?"

"Yeah, why is everything alright?"

"No, yeah, everything is good. It's just that tonight's my Lesbian night and I have all these fuckin' dykes here driving me crazy. They're making out, fondling each other and two steps from sticking beer bottles up their asses. They're fuckin' beautiful."

26

"Ahhh, yes my friend, I know what you mean. I'll be there shortly."
"Okay buddy, I'll see you soon."

"I'm sorry ladies, but I gotta go. If you ladies aren't done by the time I get out of here, I'll gladly join you."

"Okay handsome, suit yourself. Byyeee."

Tony took another drag from his cigarette before he flicked it across the parking lot. He entered the club and was immediately recognized by the cashier, a beautiful Latina woman by the name of Sonia.

"Hi pa, how you doing lindo?" asked Sonia, beckoning Tony to come and hug her.

"Hey Sonia. How are you?" Tony hugged and kissed her back. *"Is Artie around?"*

"Yeah papi. He's upstairs in the office."

"Thank you ma."

"Okay papi, see you later."

Tony entered through the door and into a flock of at least 200 women clinging off each other, sprawled onto couches, occupying every corner of the club. Women were tongue tied and flanked by more women groping each other. To Tony, it felt as if at any moment, this was going to turn into one of the biggest orgies he had ever witnessed. He grabbed a stool at a bar where he was greeted by a gorgeous bartender. She had tanned skinned, a statuesque, hard body, and a head full of light brown curls that bounced with every step she took. Her name was Vicki, but they called her "V" for short. Tony had always liked V a lot, but she used to date one of Tony's friends so as far as he was concerned she was off limits.

"Hey Tone, how are you doing, you are soo beautiful" said V.

"Thank you, I'm Okay. How are you doing sweetheart?" replied Tony.

"Good. What are you having, Baily's?"

"You know what V, I started drinking Mojito and I was going to get that but, I don't know, something about the way you asked me just seduced me into getting Baily's. So, yeah, I'll have the Baily's straight up."

V looked at Tony with a slight smile.

"Tony, why haven't you ever asked me out?"

"because you were Joey's girl and I thought you were into women."

"I was Joeys girl, past tense and I am into women, but occasionally I have my beef with broccoli you know..."

"No, I didn't know. Had I known, we would've hung out. "

"Yeah honey, I get the best of both worlds – a hard solid cock when I need penetration and a gorgeous woman when I want to have my orgasmic needs met."

"Your orgasmic needs? What, a guy doesn't do that for you?"

"Well I haven't met one yet that has done it for me."

"Damn baby, you just haven't tried me yet."

"Tone, I'm gonna be honest with you. I'm afraid of you."

"Damn girl, am I that hideous?"

V laughed for a moment. "No, it's just that you seem to be like this perfect guy, and I'm a sucker for that stuff. I know myself and I could easily fall in love with you."

"And that's a bad thing?" asked Tony.

"Well yeah, it's a bad thing when after like 3 months, you're no longer the way you were at the beginning. That's why I got into girls, because there's not as much drama and I can't fall in love with a girl, therefore I can't get hurt."

"Wow V, I didn't know you felt that way about me. I don't know if that's a compliment or a bad thing. Either way, thank you, but I think you're issue is with the guys you trusted in the past. Not all guys are the same. I know you hear that a lot from guys wanting to get into your pants and all, but some guys are real gentlemen."

"Do you want to get in my pants?" asked V.

Tony laughed. *"Of course V."*

"See what I mean Tone?"

"Look V, who wouldn't want to get in your pants? Excuse my French, but you're fucking fine babe."

"Thank you" replied V. *"Just promise me that if we go out one day, you won't seduce me."*

"I promise baby. But what is it that a woman does for you anyway?"

"Not much different than what a guy does. You see, a woman knows exactly where and how another woman wants to be held, touched, and played with. She knows how to get another woman's juices flowing."

"I see, you've got all the bases covered then, huh?"

"All except you baby."

A petite young lady who walked up to order drinks suddenly distracted Tony.

" Two Apple Martinis please" said the girl.

She was about 5' 4", with honey-colored hair, olive-skinned, and had one of the best asses Tony had seen in the club that night. Her face was adorned with the cutest set of almond eyes and a plump set of lips. V returned with her drinks, and Tony called her over to see him.

"Daammmnn, put it on my tab V."

"Why don't you take her home tonight Tone? What do you think?" V laughed.

"How much?" asked the girl walking over to V.

"Oh don't worry honey. See that hot guy over there." V pointed to where Tony sat. *"He already paid for it."*

Tony was watching her on the reflection of the mirror behind the bar. He hadn't looked at her directly, but he was sure she'd head his way – at least to say thank you for the drink. He watched her from the mirror and saw her looking at him, contemplating over whether or not she should say something. After a while, she finally decided to walk over.

"Thank you."

Tony replied, *"You're welcome."*

He then turned around and faced the crowd, while leaning nonchalantly on the bar. Tony pretended not to be interested, and only peeped at the girl's curvaceous body.

"Magnificent view" said Tony.
The girl smiled and said, *"Yes it is."*

Her beautiful almond shaped eyes and pixie-like eyelashes batted flirtatiously. Her beauty had a beguiling purity to it that was magnified by the glow of the evening club lights.

Torn

"What in particular do you enjoy about this view?" she asked.

"Oh sweety, the same thing you do, seeing as how we both love women."

She smiled, stuck out her hand and said, *"My friends call me Inez."*

Tony took her hand into his own and replied, *"Antonio Falcon, but my friends call me Tony."*

They shook hands. V tapped Tony on the shoulder.

"Need anything hun?" she asked.

"Yeah, let me have a mojito."

"Mojito, what is that?" asked Inez.

"It's a Cuban drink made from 2 oz. of light rum, 1 oz. of lime juice, 2 teaspoons of sugar, a small handful of spearmint, and seltzer water in a tall glass."

"Mmmmm, sounds delicious. You a bartender too?"

"Yeah, I've tended bar before."

"Well Antonio, it's been a real pleasure meeting you." She reached out to shake his hand, which he took into his own.

"You have no idea" he replied.

They smiled at each other and as she walked away, his eyes stood glued to her posterior. It was an incredible sight for him. He had to have her. She would be his, but how? He thought about it for a while as he stood in a trance. V snapped him back to reality.

"Damn boy!" said V. Tony started laughing.

31

"What?" he asked.

"So that's your type, huh?" asked V.

"Well V, I'm a sucker for lips and she's got a pair that are driving me crazy."

"Look at me Tone." V grabbed her silicone rack, pressed them together and held them up toward him. *"Tell me again, do you find me attractive?"*

"Of course I find you attractive. You're beautiful."

"So why..."

"Because V, you work here and I run the shows here. With all the guys who hit on you and all the girls that hit on me, it's just a recipe for disaster and drama in the workplace which won't do any of us any good."

She gave Tony a nasty look.

"Don't flatter yourself. I don't want a relationship. I just want to fuck."

Tony laughed as she walked away to serve the next customer. He swung around in his stool and saw his big-lipped beauty grinding away on the dance floor with a waif, skinny-looking model type while balancing her apple martini. He started disrobing her with his eyes, when at the distant rear of the club he saw an arm waving that broke him out of his trance. He looked over and saw his co-worker Rick.

Tony and Rick were both part-time Verizon technicians. Tony waved back and immediately got up and made his way to the back of the club to greet Rick. They gave each other a partnerly hug.

"Yo Tone, what's up?"

"What's up buddy?"

"Hey Tone, this is my friend Ray and his wife Gina."

Tony greeted Ray, a huge Italian white boy who looked like was jacked on steroids. His wife Gina, also an Italian, was a knockout. He sat down and Ray immediately got up and waved over a waitress. He ordered two bottles of Don Perignon.

"Tony buddy, you want a hit?" Ray asked.

"No, no, no I'm good. Champagne will be good, thanks."

"Alright buddy, how about my wife?"

"Your wife?" Tony asked, wondering if he misheard Rob. He glanced over at Rick and Rick laughed, so he laughed too.

"What do you mean your wife?"

As he waited for a response, Tony stared at him, not knowing if he was serious or joking. Ray looked at his wife and patted his knee, beckoning for his wife to sit down. She got up, sat on his lap, and started making out intensely. Tony glanced over at Rick, unsure of what to think of the situation. Rick simply smiled and shrugged back. Tony knew something was up. He looked over at the couple and saw that they were still making out. Ray slowly slipped his hand over her perfectly round breast and underneath her skin-tight dress. He pulled out one of her breasts and sucked on it. He looked up at Tony with her exposed breast pointing straight at him.

Tony thought to himself for a moment. *"What the fuck is this shit?"* he wondered.

"Tony, you like my wife's tits?" asked Ray.

"Uh huh. They're really nice Rob" replied Tony.

33

"They better be. They fucking cost me seven grand buddy. Go ahead, give them a squeeze."

"Na that's okay bro, maybe later."

The fiasco hadn't gone unnoticed however. Three minutes later, a Bouncer walked over.

His 6' 5" frame bent low over our table.

"Guys do me a favor, the girl has to stay dressed, okay?" said the Bouncer.

"Sorry about that Joe. We didn't mean nothing by it. We'll cool down." Tony said. The bouncer left shortly after.

"What are you doing tonight Tony?"

"Nothing really. Just gonna take care of a little business then I'm free. Why?"

"Well we're gonna go to my place and party a little. There probably gonna be a couple of other people there. You should come for a while. Rick's gonna come."

"Yeah Rick, you going?"

Rick nodded.

"Yeah sure, just gimme half an hour" replied Tony.

Tony got up and deliberately crossed the dance floor, dodging and weaving his way all around the beautiful women. His mission was to somehow get a second meeting with his scrumptious lipped Inez. He spotted her at the bar and made his move. He leaned on the bar and said, *" Man, if I were a girl, you'd be mine."*

"Really?" she said, surprised by his confidence.

"Yes, you would so be mine."

They gave each other a long, intense stare.

"Well why do you think you have to be a girl for me to be yours? What makes you think I'm a lesbian?"

"Well, for starters, you are here and tonight is lesbian night. Number two, I saw you dancing real close with that other model looking girl. Now is she going to be upset if she sees us speaking?"

"I don't know. She's in the bathroom. But why don't we eliminate the thought of you being a girl? You look great as a man, just the way I like it" said Inez.

"Well look, I don't want to give your friend any reason to be upset, so what f I call you during the week? We'll do dinner."

"Yeah, that sounds nice" replied Inez.

When Tony turned around, he noticed V standing behind him.

"Ready V?"

"Yeah, go ahead" she replied.

"Read your number to the bartender" Tony told Inez.

"917-415-0127"

"Got it" said V.

"So then I hope to..."

"You hope to what?" Tony turned around only to come face to face with the model girl that was with Inez.

Tony looked at her and relied, *"I was saying that I hope you and your girlfriend have a good night. That's all."*

The girl came around, grabbed Inez, and led her to the dance floor.

Tony looked over at V and they both started laughing.

"That was a close one" said Tony.

"You see, why go through all that drama when you can have all of this?" asked V.

"The thrill of the hunt V, the thrill of the hunt…"

"Well Mr. Thrill, take this number before I call this hottie myself and do the deed."

She passed him the number and Tony returned to the table where Ray, Rick, and Gina were.

"Everyone ready?" asked Ray.

They all got up and Gina started giving Tony an intense stare. Tony smiled and tried to break the intensity as they exited Mystiques.

'So Tone, what do you like drinking?" asked Ray.

"Oh, pretty much anything, but when I'm relaxing, a little Godiva White puts me right."

"Nice choice" said Ray.

The group loaded up in Ray's Lexus and drove up to the liquor store.

"How about you Rick, the usual?"

"Yeah, Rob, Stoli, and Club." replied rick

He shut the car door and headed inside. Tony looked at Rick and asked, *"Yo bro, what's going on bro. Why do I feel like I'm in the dark here?"*

Rick laughed again.

"I don't know bro."

"Where do you know these people from?"

"Oh man, I've known them for years. They're cool people Tone, just relax."

"Alright bro."

Ray got in, threw the shopping bags at Tony and Rick, and drove off. Tony watched as Ray pulled into a mini-mart to get some gas. Leaving the gas gun in the gas hole, Ray headed into the store and asked the cashier for something. The cashier reached up on a shelf and placed about eight boxes of condoms on top of the counter. Tony watched as she put them into a bag and charged him. Soon after, Ray walked back to the car and surrendered the gas nozzle, got in the car, and drove off.

After a forty-minute drive, the group pulled up to a gated community where an access card granted them entry into a set of waterfront condos. They parked, exited the vehicle, headed upstairs, and entered the condo. Tony looked around and noticed a very clean, eclectic place adorned with top of the line furniture, equipment, and beautiful vaulted ceilings complete with a stained glass skylight.

"Guys make yourself at home. Prep the drinks, I'm gonna get comfortable."

Ray and Gina left both of them in the living room and headed back to what seemed to be the master bedroom.

"Rick, what's going on bro?"

"Nothing bro." Rick laughed, but Tony had the feeling that something was going on and he was purposely being left out of the loop.

"So why do you keep laughing every time I ask you?"

"Bro, because you're so freakin' paranoid bro. Just go make the drinks and relax already, okay?" He laughed again.

"Ok bro" replied Tony.

Rick grabbed the remote and dimmed the lights. With another click of the remote, the fireplace roared to life. Tony was amazed of the technology. Another click turned on the stereo that began to spit out techno tunes. Rick and Tony were drinking, laughing, and taking shots, when Rick nodded his head at Tony, signaling for him to look behind him. When Tony turned around, what he saw almost knocked him on his ass. Gina was standing there in six-inch heels, white stockings complete with lace and garter belts, white thong and no bra. Her perfectly shaped breasts hung perfectly on her chest. She looked absolutely flawless. All of a sudden, Rick burst out in laughter again.

"Surprise" said Rick.

Tony looked back at Gina, still stunned. He didn't know whether to smile or be serious. She opened the refrigerator door, grabbed herself a beer, and walked her sexy fuckin' ass back toward the bedroom. Tony jumped up and tipped-toed toward the corridor. He peeked at her and saw her prancing back toward the room. Her beautiful ass swayed from side-to-side with just a slight jiggle.

Tony turned back around to find Rick grabbing his stomach trying to ease the pain of the intense laughter he was having at Tony's expense.

Tony said, *"You fuck, you knew this was going to happen all along, didn't you? My god she's fuckin' beautiful bro! What's going on?*

Where's Ray?"

"He'll be here my friend. Just relax and enjoy."

Five minutes later Ray emerged wearing Boxer Briefs and carrying a briefcase. He set it on the huge glass table and popped it open to reveal a sandwich bag with what appeared to be cocaine in it. He set it out on the table as if he was setting out party favors. Next to that he set out brown pills, blue, pills, white pills, and a small bottle with a clear liquid. He bent over, and using a nail file, he snorted the cocaine. Rick followed Ray and did the same.

"Come on Tone. Take a hit."

"Na man, I'm good. I'm straight. I'm just drinking tonight guys."

Ray and Rick looked over Tony's shoulders, Tony turned around to see what was there, and saw Gina again, still prancing around half-naked. Noticing that everyone else was smiling, Tony smiled too. Gina put her arm around Ray and started making out with him. As she did, Ray palmed both her ass cheeks and swung her around so that her back was facing Tony. Not knowing the etiquette for the situation, Tony pushed himself and his stool further back away from them, just watching what appeared to be a live version of the porn DVD he usually watched. Ray picked her up by the waist and set her down on the white shag rug that adorned their living room floor. He positioned her on all fours, facing Tony, and moved in behind her.

Ray got on his knees and began hammering her from behind. All the while, she stared at Tony with a "come fuck me look". As Ray hammered and hammered away at her, her tits swung back and forth in the same direction as her hair. Tony turned to Rick to see if he was enjoying this as much as he was , but he had his face buried in the white powder, snorting it up.

Suddenly, Ray stopped and looked at Tony as if he had done something wrong. Tony's mind started racing,

"Oh shit what did I do? Did I stare to hard? Was I supposed to look away? Shit!"

"Hey Tony", said Ray.

Tony swallowed hard, almost as if he was swallowing rocks.
"You gonna help me out here or what?"

"Huh?" asked Tony. Fear had him bewildered by the situation.

"Come on bro, I need a little help here." Tony glanced down at Gina who was beckoning him with her finger.

"Oh boy", thought Tony. Ray resumed his banging, and Tony walked up to Gina, obeying her command.

"Take off your pants and put your cock in my mouth" she commanded.

"What?" thought Tony to himself, despite having clearly heard her.

All he could think about at the moment was that while this woman's husband was banging her from behind, and she was blowing on him, her husband might suddenly plunge a knife through his chest. "Oh my God" he thought. Slowly, Tony started to undo his belt, but was shaking so much that it looked as if he drank a gallon of coffee. She reached up with her right hand, grabbed Tony's pants, and pulled them down just as he unzipped them.

With her left hand, she pulled down Tony's underwear exposing his tool. Then again with her right hand, she wrapped her pretty little fingers around his huge member and placed it in her mouth. She started to glide her mouth back and forth on Tony's cock, giving a shiny wet coat of saliva. He placed his hands on her head and interlaced his fingers through her hair. Tony looked down at her and the only thing that moved aside from her swaying tits, were her gorgeous green eyes staring right at him.

Tony looked away at Rick, who was now sitting on the table snorting his ass away. When he looked up at him, his whole nose and upper lip were white. He exposed a smile that revealed his pearly white teeth and gave Tony a thumbs up. Tony looked back at Ray who was slaving away at his wife. Suddenly, Ray stopped and pointed at him as if to say "your turn". He got up off his knees and walked away toward the bedroom.

Tony walked around Gina and watched her as she arched her back, and puckered up her cute little ass like a cat in heat. He looked at her exposed pink bud, lubricated with so much of her own juices that her inner thighs were dripping wet. Tony reached over to the couch, into the grocery bag, and pulled out one of the boxes of condoms. He opened it up, took one out, and tore open the wrapper. Tony put on the condom and approached the masterpiece of an ass that was in front of him.

He grabbed her waist and positioned her so that her ass was even more arched than she originally had it. Then, he grabbed her right ass cheek with his right hand, her left ass cheek with his left hand, and making sure that both thumbs were facing in, he spread them as if he were opening a head of lettuce. She looked back at him and said, "Tony, put it in baby."

Tony put the head of his penis into her ripe flower. She moaned and pulled herself forward as if it hurt her. She slowly pushed back, to feel more of his pole, only to stop and pull forward again.

"Are you okay?"

"Yeah, I just have to get used to you." She smiled, turned her head, and thrust herself back to Tony again. He kept his pace, trying not to hurt her and stared at the beads of sweat glistening on her back. Then, Tony saw something with the corner of his eye. He saw somebody pointing something at him, and feared that his previous vision was becoming a reality.

"Fuck it" he told himself. He just kept going and going, ramming

41

and ramming, getting more and more aggressive with each passing minute. *"If I'm gonna die, I'm gonna die banging a beautiful doll of a woman."* Her cried started to get louder as his thrusts got more violent. The vision didn't seem to be backing down either. On the contrary it came closer and closer. Tony's body was drenched in sweat, the fear emanating through his pores, but he kept banging away until Gina finally let out a climatic cry.

"Aaaahhh, shit! I'm coming, I'm coming!"

She exploded all over Tony's hard cock. The thrusts came to a standstill. The music kept thumping and when Tony finally looked up at the vision, he saw Ray standing there, stark naked, with a video camera in his hand. Tony dropped to the floor like a wet rag.

"Tony, that was great bro", said Ray while handing him a drink. Tony took a sip and let out a sigh of relief. Gina ran her fingers through his hair.

"That was amazing Tony."

Tony watched as she got up, went over to Ray, and melted in the arms of her husband.

Not knowing the etiquette involved in doing this kind of thing, Tony sat there drinking and trying to piece together what had just happened.

"How do I leave? Do I just get up and go? Say bye? Would it be rude to just leave without the chit-chat? Do we go at it again?"

He lifted his arm and checked his watch, hopeful that the couple would take the hint that he was thinking about leaving. Instead, Ray brought him another drink. Tony looked up to see Rick dancing with Gina. Ray watched in the wing, and smiled as his wife enjoyed herself. Tony politely declined to more offers of hits of white powder. Ray crossed Tony and headed back toward the bedroom, but not before tapping him on the shoulder and motioning for him to follow him. Tony got up and followed Ray to his bedroom, where he shut the door.

"What's up Ray?" asked Tony.

"My wife really likes you."

Tony opened up his eyes and squinted again, trying to differentiate what part of this conversation was real and what part was lost to all the shot and drinks that he had, had earlier with Rick.

"Your wife really likes me?"

"Yeah, she told me."

Tony could not believe he was telling him this.

"Ok Ray, how can I help?"

Ray laughed. Tony tried to figure out what the hell was so funny about the situation.

"I like you Tone. You seem like a real cool guy. Our friend Rick told me you were a real straight-up guy and I just seem to feel that we can all amplify each ' lives. You see Tone, I love my wife and there isn't anything I wouldn't do for her, including, as you saw tonight, giving her another man."

"I'm not gay bro", replied Tony.

"Neither am I Tone, but there's nothing I enjoy more than watching my wife getting fucked by someone other than myself. Let me see how I can put this so that you'd understand. Okay look, you've seen a Ferrari, right?"

"Yeah" replied Tony, still dumfounded by the situation.

"Well I'm sure you've seen that car zip down the highway. It looks

43

awesome and the car is fun to look at, but when you open the door to a Ferrari and get inside, you don't really see the car anymore. It sort of disappears until you stop at a red light and look over at a reflection on a huge window store—that's when you see the car. Then when you drive off the car is gone again, until you park it and you see it again while walking away from it. Well, it's sort of the same thing with my wife. It excites me more to watch my wife making those faces and hearing those moans as she's getting fucked, than me actually doing it."

"I see", said Tony. He kind of understood what he meant by that, but he wasn't about to get married and let some dude bang the shit out of his wife.

"So Tone, this is what I would like if it's okay with you. Maybe sometime next week we'll get together, you, me, and my wife?"

"What about Rick?" asked Tony.

"Nah, Rick can sit this one out. What do you say?" asked Rick. He held out his hand towards Tony, and Tony shook it in return,

"Okay Ray, I'd be glad to."

Ray put his arm around Tony and said *"Alright buddy!"* It was as if he had just won the lottery. The two of them left the room and joined Rick and Gina, who were dancing, drinking, and snorting.

"A toast!" said Ray, happier than Tony had seen him all night. He served everyone shots, to which they all raised their glasses. After finishing their drinks, Rick moved to serve the group some more drinks.

"One more!" he yelled.

"No, no, no I've gotta run. It's four in the morning", said Tony.

"Hold on Tone", said Ray, "Let me get you a cab. In the meantime

you can have one more shot."

"Damn" Tony said to himself, "This guy's outta control."

Tony made his way to the bathroom, shut the door, and leaned over to look at his reflection in the mirror. He smiled to himself.

"You lucky motherfucker. I can't believe this fuckin' shit just happened", he said to himself.

Tony opened the faucet and splashed cold water on his face trying to wash away the dizziness. When he looked back into the mirror, he found himself startled to see Gina standing behind him. She pushed up against him and crossed her hand over his pelvis and onto the front of his pants. She started to rub his dick over his pants and felt his penis pulsating. It was getting bigger and harder. Tony knew that if he'd let it continue, he'd never leave. Instead he turned around and ended up in her arms. He kissed her on the forehead.

"Sweetie, I've gotta go", said Tony.

"Okay baby, when will we see you again?" asked Gina.

"Next week sometime. I'll set it up with your husband."

"Okay, hun."

They left the bathroom and Tony headed for the door.

"Okay fellas, I'm outta here. Rick I'll see you at work. Ray it's been a real pleasure meeting you bro. You have a beautiful wife."

"No Tone, the pleasure was literally all ours."

They both smiled and Tony left.

****

Tony got up and started to get ready for his lunch meeting with George at J.P.'s. Tony entered the restaurant and was seated by the host at the usual balcony spot.

"Your waitress will be right with you", said the Host.

"Thank you", replied Tony.
He sat there and stared over the City Island waters at the bridge, waiting to see the yellow beast cross over. He heard the angelic voice.

"One pitcher of fruity sangria. You're waiting for your partner, so you won't order, and I didn't get your name the last time you were here. You left so fast."

Tony flashed a smile from ear to ear and slowly turned his head.

"Well hello Kristina, Oh, I'm sorry. Can I call you Kristy?", asked Tony.

"Sure, all of my friends call me Kristy", replied the pretty waitress.

"Well Kristy, my name is Tony."

"So Tony, was I right with the order?" asked Kristina.

"Yes, you were precisely right with the order. Thank you."

"Okay, be right back with your sangria."

"Sure."

Tony looked over at the bridge and saw the yellow beast cross over. Five minutes later, George walked in with pricey duds as he was the night of the club. Tony admired his style, which was very similar to his own. Tony got up, shook hands with George, and sat back down.

"Here's your Sangria guys, enjoy. Let me know when you're ready

to order" said Kristy.

"Okay, thank you Kristy. By the way Kristy, this is George."

"Hello Kristy, nice meeting you" said George.

"Likewise George" replied Christie.

Tony poured the Sangria. George grabbed the sugar and held it up over the pitcher.

"What the hell is this guy doing?" Tony thought.

George knew what Tony was thinking.

"The more sugar it has, the quicker it gets to your head."

"Oh okay, so what's up?" Tony asked.

"Did you think about my proposition."

"Well I did manage to give it some thought, but not as much as I would've liked to. I was pretty tied up last night with this guy and his wife. It was pretty crazy."

"What do you mean his wife?" asked George.

"Well yeah man, it was the weirdest thing. I met them through my work partner. We went to their house last night and ended up making some sort of porn film."

"What?!" George shouted in excitement.

"Yeah bro, it was completely unexpected."

"Damn bro, you should've called me."

"I couldn't", replied Tony, *"I didn't know what was going to happen*

myself. It all happened too fast. We had some drinks and before I knew it, everyone was naked, the camera was rolling, I was taking his wife from behind, and my boy was snorting a shitload of coke."

"Coke? George asked.

"Yeah Coke, GHB, Oxycontin, Viagra, Weed, all that shit."

"Who does this guy get his stuff from?"

"I don't know bro. I met them yesterday. I didn't even know they did that shit until they pulled out a mountain full that shit and threw it on the glass table. Why do you ask?"

"Ah nothing, just curious. Anyway Tone, I'd like for you to come on board with me on this club thing. I'm even willing to sweeten the deal for you."

"What do you mean sweeten the deal?"

"Well, I'm thinking I'll acquire the club with my own cash, nothing out of your pocket. I'll make you my partner as head entertainment and bar staff manager, pay you $500 a week cash, and 25% off all profits. Oh and a little bonus incentive, I've got in mind.

What do you think?"

"What's the extra bonus?" asked Tony.

"Well let's just say, there won't be a need for you to be taking cabs anymore."

"Yeah?"

"Yeah, you'll like it." George stuck his hand out.

"Deal?" asked George.

Torn

"Deal bro." Tony reached over the table and shook his hand.

"You guys ready to order?"

"Yes, yes."

"What would you like?"

"I'll have a dozen baked clams, steamers, steamed scallops, two lobsters, and another pitcher of sangria" said Tony.

"How about you George?" she asked.

"No, I'll be sharing what he ordered. Thank you."

"No problem guys, be right back with your order."

The food soon arrived, succulent mouth-watering juicy lobster, the biggest and best-tasting clams on all of City Island, and steamers and scallops worth dying for. They ate and drank for hours, joking around and enjoying their newfound partnership. George looked at Tony and noticed his glossy eyes and drunken smile. George knew Tony was a drinking lightweight and enjoyed the drinking battle that they were having. Little did they know that they were being ogled and watched by the waitress staff from behind the waitress way-station.

"Ooooh, they look cute together", said one of the waitresses.

"Look at them, I think they're so brave for coming out of the closet like that."

"They look so happy together."

Kristy was flagged down by the guys.

"Yes?" asked Kristy

49

"We'll take the check please."

Kristy left the check at the table.

"Thank you gentlemen, have a good night."

"Good night sweetheart", said Tony while smiling at her in a half-drunken state.

"How much bro?" asked Tony.

George laughed and shook his head. He knew Tony couldn't even count his own money in the state he was in.

"Don't worry, I got it bro."

Tony watched as George pulled out two one hundred dollar bills and left them on the table with the check.

"Tone you alright?" asked George.

Tony stammered and answered, *"Yeah, yeah bro, never better bro."*

He got up, lost his balance, and landed right back in his seat. They both started laughing. George looked at him, shook his head, and said, *"Yeah right lightweight, let's go."*

He grabbed Tony's arm and helped him into his car. Tony pressed his forehead against the window and watched as Christina picked up the money and check. He saw the apparent shock on her face from seeing the large tip.

The yellow beast roared off into the distance and Tony's head turned back, slowly following her face, as it became a speck in the distance.

"Bro, I'm in love", Tony said half-drunk.

"In love?"

Torn

" With who?"

"With a waitress" Tony said.

George laughed. *"Well why didn't you say anything?"*

"Well, rapping on a beautiful girl like that is never a good thing when you're drunk. Your breath smells like liquor, your speech is slurred, and when you walk, you look like a sleepy slop of shit and nobody fucking says anything. Women don't like that fucking shit bro. They right away get the fucking wrong impression and you only get one fucking shot to make a fucking good first impression."

George looked at Tony and laughed.

"What the fuck you laughing at?" asked Tony.

"Are you aware of how much you use the word "fuck" when you're drunk?" asked George.

"Really?" asked Tony.

"Yeah partner, it's bad", replied George.

Tony remained silent, and when George looked over, the conversation was cut short. The rest of the ride was quiet.

"Tone, wake up buddy."

George shook Tony until he opened his eyes.

"Oh shit, we're here", said Tony.

"Yeah bro, you fell asleep talking about first impressions."

"I was probably talking shit, eh?"

"Nah, nah, you made a lot of sense and you've got a point."

51

"Okay bud, I'm outta here", said Tony.
Tony got out of the car and made his way into the building.

****

Six months passed and George and Tony not only became partners, but also the best of friends. They visited and scouted about sixty locations for the club. During that time, Tony had visited Ray and Gina about eight times, with each time crazier than the last.

J.P.'s became Tony and George's restaurant of choice not only because of the five star meals, but also because the women there were incredibly beautiful—customers and waitresses alike. They were frequenting the restaurant four days a week. With every visit, the owner would come from behind the kitchen to greet them and their drinks were always on the house. They got to know all the waitresses on a first name basis.

Tony had approximately two conversations with Inez. By the third conversation, he was ready to meet her, but as fate would have it—it would not be. Between work, meeting up with George for business, visiting J.P.'s, and performing his strip shows, there really wasn't time for much else.

RING RING RING

'Hello"

"Happy Birthday buddy", said George.

"Hey, hey, what's up buddy? Thank you", said Tony.

"What are you doing today?" asked George.

"I'm here with my partner Rick. We're hooking up a phone line for a customer on 67th street", replied Tony.

"Some way to spend your birthday. You should've taken the day off",

said George.

"Nah, I've gotta work man. I gotta make this money."

"Friday night buddy, it's your birthday and we're celebrating tonight."
"Where are we going?"

"Don't worry bro. Just be ready by six."

"A-ight buddy."

Tony arrived and at home and started to get ready for the night out.

The intercom buzzed to life.

"Yeah?" called out Tony through the intercom.

"Hey I'm downstairs, come down" crackled George's voice through the speaker.

"Okay."

Tony went downstairs and saw the yellow beast rumbling out in front. He walked around the front of the car, got in, and they took off.

"So where are we going?" asked Tony.

"I figured we go to our usual spot at J.P.'s, get a bite, some drinks, then we'll head out to Mystique's for a couple of hours—see if we get lucky."

Tony laughed.

"Yeah alright, sounds good."

A few minutes later they pulled into J.P.'s parking lot and entered the restaurant. Three waitresses greeted them at the door. After seating them, the owner personally stepped over to Tony and George's table.

"Tony, George, good evening guys. How are you gentlemen tonight?"

"Great John, what's new?"

"What's new is the two waitresses I hired on Wednesday. They're twins and they're gorgeous. I'll send them over with your drinks—on me guys."

"Thank you John."

Five minutes later, in walked two of the most gorgeous twins they had ever seen. One carried a pitcher of sangria and the other carried two cups. They stood in front of the table and said, in unison, *"Good evening, welcome to J.P.'s. These drinks are on the house. If you need to anything, our names are Jessie and Becky."*

"Wow, music to my ears. Thank you ladies. You both are beautiful. I am Tony and this is George."

Tony motions towards George.

They all greeted each other and the twins made their way out. John had been one hundred percent correct in his assessment of their beauty. They were hot.

A couple of minutes later...

"Hello guys, are you having the usual?"

Tony looked up. *"Jesus she's so beautiful"*, he thought to himself.

"Yes, the usual. Thank you Kristy"

"No problem" she responded, and walked away.

Torn

"Hey Tone, I would really like to see you in action. I want to see you get this girl", George said.

"I don't know George man. I'm not doubting myself, but she's so fine. She makes any guy doubt himself. I haven't really seen a clear signal that she's interested."

"Here are your drinks guys. Be back shortly with your order", said Kristy, arriving a few moments later.

"Thank you Kristy."

"No problem."

Tony glanced at George.

"You see man, she's like a robot man—nothing, I can't get a reading."

George laughed.

"Yo bro, she is beautiful."

"I know bro, I'll figure something out."

"Tone I'll be back. I'm going to the bathroom."

George left and Tony picked up the phone to call Rick.

RING RING

"Hello?"

"Yo Rick?"

"Yeah."

"It's me Tony."

"How's the B-day boy?"

"Good bro. Hey you want to join me tonight to celebrate?"

"Fuck yeah bro!" said George excitedly. *"Anything for you!"*

"Hey call Ray and let him know it's my B-day. Tell him to come with you. I want to see him there."

"Okay, what time?"

"Be there at midnight."

"Done buddy."

"Okay, see you there."

Tony hung up the phone and filled his glass with more sangria. He gulped it down.

"Hey, drinking without me?"

"Hey I called my friend Rick and he's meeting us over there."
"Gentlemen, here's your food, your baked clams, your lobster, your steamers, and steamed scallops. Anything else?", said Kristy.

"We're good for now, thank you", Tony said.

They started to eat and enjoyed the night. The clock approached 11 p.m. and Tony was already half-drunk. George was a little tipsy, but could handle double of what Tony drank.

"Hey, kill that last cup and I'll be right back."

Tony began to pour the last bit of sangria. As he did, an eruption of voices caused him to spill the remaining sangria all over the table.

"Happy Birthday to you, Happy Birthday to you...."

When he looked up, it was the whole entire waitress staff singing. Kristy was up front holding the cake and smiling. Tony looked at Kristy who was just radiating, and the candlelight shimmered off her cheeks. He wasn't sure if it was real or not. The only reason he knew it was real, was because of the ice and red sangria he had spilled all over his lap. Tony was cold, stained and excited when he saw kristy holding a cake for him. She placed it on the table. George slid back into the booth and smiled at him.

"Make a wish", said George.

Tony looked at George, then at all the beauties, and made his wish. He blew out all the candles and the place erupted in applause. Each waitress lined up, kissed Tony on the cheek, and said their *"Happy Birthdays"*.

"Hey Tone, you alright? Cause we gotta go bro", said George.

George had already taken care of the bill. He had done so during one of his many bathroom trips. George shoved a fifty-dollar bill in Tony's hand.

"Here bro, give this to your baby. I'll wait in the car."

Tony started to walk away when he saw Kristy. He waved at her and signaled for her to come over. He handed her the fifty and smiled.

"Thank you again beautiful."

"No, no, no. This is too much. I can't take that", she said.

Tony turned away and walked out. He jumped into the car that was waiting outside and both he and George sped off into the distance. Tony noticed that they were headed towards Manhattan. Club Mystique, however, was in the Bronx.

****

"Hey, where the hell are we going?"

"We need to buy you some clothes. Look at you, you're a mess."

"It's 11:30 at night. Where the hell are we going to find a store at this hour?"

"Don't worry buddy, just leave that to me", said George.

"Okay", said Tony.

They drove to 174th street and Broadway. He popped a U-turn and pulled right up to what looked like a boutique. George picked up his phone and punched a few numbers.

"Oye! Estoy aqui, abre la puerta."

"Okay", said a voice over the phone.

"Let's go", said George.

They got out of the car and approached the boutique. The window display had mannequins sporting expensive brand name clothing. A small, olive-skinned man opened the door to let George in. The two exchanged a friendly hug.

"Dimelo mi pana, que tal?"

"Bien, bien. Oye visteme al hermano mio que se ramo todo el trago ensime."

"Esta bien."

"Raphy this is Tony", said George, finally introducing the two men to each other.

Raphy took one look at Tony, made some hand gestures as if he were making calculations, and sent Tony into the dressing room. Three minutes later, Raphy came back and handed Tony a brand new pair of light blue Versace pants, with a silk |Prada shirt, and a pair of D&G slip-ons in leather. Tony noticed the tags had been ripped off. The suit fit Tony perfectly.

"Coño you look like a superstar man."

"Thank you", said Tony. *"How much Raphy?"* asked Tony.

"Oh no, hoy es tu cumpleano. Es tu regalo", said Raphy.

"Hey George how much is this so I can pay this guy?"

"Tone didn't you hear him. Happy Birthday man. It's your birthday gift."

"George seriously bro, how much did this set you back?"

"I don't know bro, $900-$2000. Who cares bro? You look great."

"What $900? Are you fuckin' nuts?"

"Look Tone, you're gonna learn that it's better to buy a quality designer shirt at $500 than five shirts at $100 each. They just last longer and nothing else will give you that feeling of knowing you are wearing a top quality $500 shirt. Don't you feel better now than when you left your house?"

Tony admitted to himself that he felt rather incredible.

"Yeah I feel great. I even feel a little cocky knowing that I am wearing clothes that are more expensive than like 98% of the people that we'll be encountering tonight."

He felt great.

****

Tony and George pulled into the parking lot at Mystiques, got out, and went inside. The bouncer acknowledged their presence and let them in.

"Happy Birthday Tone", said the bouncer.
"Thank you Joe", replied Tony.

They walked in and Artie snuck up from behind. He put his arm around Tony's shoulder.

"How old are you now birthday boy? 50?

Artie laughed.

"George what's up baby?"

"Fuck you old man", said Tony jokingly.

They both hugged and laughed.

"Guys your friends are waiting for you at the V.I.P. tables. Tony, drinks are on me buddy. Happy Birthday buddy!"

"Thank you Artie."

"Later Artie", said George.

Tony and George headed to the V.I.P. section of the club. Tony spotted Rick and walked over to him. He shook Rob's hand and bent over to give Gina a kiss on the cheek. Immediately, however, she grabbed Tony's face and pressed her lips roughly against his.

Tony smiled and introduced George to everyone else.

"Guys this is George. George this is Ray, Rick, and Gina."

George shook all of their hands and gave Tony a look of approval, with regards to Gina. George tried to keep his composure in front of

Gina, but her beauty was too much for him. He just stared. Tony took notice and discreetly jammed his heel into George's toes.

"Oww!", said George.

"Stop staring bro!"

Ray grabbed the champagne bottle and filled everyone's cup. He lifted up his glass.

"To the birthday boy!" he yelled.

Gina got up and sat on Tony's lap, giving him an instant erection. Tony glanced over at Ray who held his glass up to him. Tony smiled nervously as Gina wiggled her ass, trying to feel all of Tony's erection. She kissed him on the forehead and raised her glass.

"Cheers!" Gina shouted.

"Cheers!" they all responded.

George leaned over and whispered in Tony's ear.

"Hey that's the husband and wife from the other night?"

Tony looked over at George and nodded silently.

"Bro, she's sitting all over your cock bro, what's that about?"

"I don't know bro – it must be the clothes."

They both laughed.

"George, what would you do if she came on to you?"

He looked at Tony as if wishing that would happen.

"Yeah right, I wish."

"Be careful what you wish for", said Tony.

George stared at Tony.

"Why do you say that?'

"No reason, just repeating what you said to me at J.P.'s about the Porsche. Be careful what you wish for, that is what you said, right?"

"Yup, that's what I said."

"Hey Tony, let's dance", *said Gina.*

"Yeah, yeah, go enjoy yourself birthday boy", said Rob.

"Okay", said Tony.

Gina grabbed Tony's hand, pulled him up from the sofa, and led him onto the dance floor. She went into a sort of trance, swaying her body to the beat of the music. Her movements were that of a snake, responding to the snake charmer's music. Tony looked over to the V.I.P. area and saw Ray sitting with an arm around George. Rick was sitting there laughing his ass off as usual. Gina danced away, rubbing her waist, breasts, and pussy against Tony. All the while, Tony watched as Ray whispered something into George's ear.

"What the hell could Rob be telling him? They just met", Tony thought.

The song ended and Tony grabbed Gina by the arm.

"Come on Gina, let's get some champagne."

Tony headed back to the table, trying not to make it seem too obvious.

"Fellas, fellas, what's going on here? Break up the huddle, eh?"

Torn

Tony sat in between Ray and George.

"Hey Tone, where have you been hiding this guy George—he's a trip."
George looked at Tony and smiled. The hours passed away as they danced, laughed, and drank.

"Hey birthday boy, let's take this party to my house", said Rob.

"Fuck it, yeah. Let's go!" said Tony.

Tony stood up and scanned the dance floor for George. He saw him dancing with Gina. Tony flagged them both down with a wave of his arm. He could tell by the look in his eyes and his smile, that George was having a fantastic time. Tony knew what was to happen and he figured it was the least he could do after George had just spent $900 on him. Tony knew the drill, liquor run, gas station, buy condoms, and it would be on. But George was in for a surprise. Tony was going to do for George what Rick did for him, surprise him.

"What's up Tone?"

"Let's go buddy."

"Where are we going?"

"To Rob's house. He's got a little party for me over there."

"Oh yeah? Let's go!"

They all rounded up and left the club.

****

Tony got into the car with George.

"Oh my God bro! She's incredible!" said George.

63

"I know, I know. Slow down tiger, she's married."

Tony saw it in his eyes; George was enamored with Gina. He went on and on about her body, her tits, her ass, and all Tony could do was smile, knowing that George would have her soon enough.

"Okay loverboy, see that Lexus?" asked Tony.

"Yeah."

"Follow it."

Both cars left the parking lot and headed towards the highway.

"What do you want to drink?" asked Tony.

"What?"

"When we pull up to the light, lower your window and tell them what you want to drink."

Both cars pulled up to the light and the windows came down.

"Hey George boy, what do you want to drink?" asked Rob.

George laughed at Tony's accurate assessment.

"Hypnotique."

"How about you Tone?" asked Rob.

"The usual buddy."

They took off liquor, gas stations, and then condoms. Tony made small talk with George so that he wouldn't notice Ray buying the condoms. He didn't want to ruin the surprise. Tony knew how perceptive George was and wondered why he was like that. That was usually a trait someone carried when they did illegal things or criminal activities. Was George a criminal? Tony thought, *"Ah, fuck it."* Tony figured he was overanalyzing George. It was a problem Tony always had- *"Why this? Why that?"*

"Hey Tony, I think Ray is planning to fuck the shit out of his wife."

"What makes you say that?"

"Cause he just bought a shitload of condoms."

Tony laughed and shook his head. Ray got in his car and took off. George followed them into the gated community. They entered and made their way upstairs to the apartment. As usual, the music ignited and the drinks started to flow. Rick and Tony looked at each other and laughed in anticipation of what was about to happen.

"What's so funny guys?" asked George.

"Nothing buddy, I'm just happy to be sharing this experience with you guys on my birthday."

Tony and Rick laughed again. Suddenly, the sound of six-inch heels coming down the foyer and into the living room revealed Gina, once again, in lingerie. George choked on the liquor that was already in his mouth. Tony patted George's back.

"You okay buddy?"

Gina appeared in a red-laced Victoria's Secret number. A red-laced half bra with the nipple portion cut out of it, complete with garter belts, and a red-laced cape. The contrast between the red outfit and her white porcelain skin was resilient. Right behind her was Ray with his black leather suitcase. After placing and opening the suitcase on the glass table, Ray revealed the usual recreational sweets that fired him up.

He pulled out the white mountain, placed it neatly on the see-through glass table, and next to that he little oxycontin, extacy, Viagra, and that same little bottle of Evian water. Tony looked at the bottle.

"Go ahead take some", said Ray.

"Water?"

"No, no, no buddy – GHB."

"No, I'm straight."

"You sure bro. Look, take a sip, swallow an oxy, and take a bump."

"Nah, nah nigga, you fuckin' nuts bro."
Ray laughed and yelled out, *"Yeah baby, you only live once!"*

Tony looked back and saw George observing from a short distance. He moved out of the way and George stepped in to observe what was being served. Tony sat down and watched the interaction of questions going on between George and Ray. Rick, on the other hand, was foaming at the mouth in anticipation of the coke party. Tony could see George making hand motions, referring to the weight and price of the drugs. Ray offered George the drugs, but he politely declined. Rick quickly accepted.

"Let's get it on buddy", said Ray.

Rick hit the table with Stoli on the rocks in one hand and a stiff dollar bill in the other. Ray stuck his nose in the white-mountain, took a swig of Vodka, and let Rick indulge.

"Yeah baby!", he yelled.

Gina approached the glass table with her little tight ass in the air. As she bent over to take a hit, Ray threw himself on his knees behind her and stuck his tongue in her pussy. She leapt up in surprise.

"Whoa! Wait honey, wait!"

She bent over again to snort and Ray continued to mop her pussy with his tongue. Tony looked over at George and his head was buried in a drink, acting as nonchalantly as possible. Tony playfully elbowed George, causing him to spill some of his drink.

"Surprise!" said Tony.

"Shit, I can't believe this is happening to me."

Yeah."

Gina looked over at Tony who was sitting next to George, and with Ray still attached to her flower hopped over and knelt in front of Tony. She slowly rubbed her hand back and forth over his hard manhood. She kept petting it with pressure until the heat from the friction made him moan. She crept up to his belt, unfastened it, and pulled out his hard, bulging cock. She held his cock up by the base right under his balls, pulled it up, and slid her mouth right over it - sucking it while simultaneously stroking it. He slid his hands under her and grabbed her huge breasts, gently pinching her nipples and looking into her eyes as she moaned in excitement.

Moans also came from underneath her where Ray was still tongue-fucking her. Tony closed his eyes and heard a third moan. When he looked over at George, he was leaning back and his eyes were closed. Gina was stroking George. Rick was in his chair, jerking himself off. Tony looked at George and offered to exchange spots with him. Tony knew George wanted to.

"Gina baby I need to go to the bathroom baby", said Tony.

"Sure honey."

Tony got up and went to the bathroom. Gina then took George into her mouth and Rick moved into Tony's seat on the couch. She now had her husband behind her, George in her mouth, and Rick in one of her free hands. Tony used the bathroom and went into the kitchen. He refilled his drink and watched the orgy unfold. Tony thought to himself about how crazy and surreal this whole situation was. Gina got up and made her way to the bedroom. Ray looked at Tony with a questioning look.

"She's sore", he whispered.

"Maybe we should take off and leave you with your wife bro."

"Nah, nah man. She's cool bro. C'mon let's do it up. Take a hit."

"Nah Ray, you should tend to your wife bro. George and I are leaving, okay?"

"You sure you don't want to do one for the road?"

"Nah I'm good bro thanks."

"How about you George?"

George had on five-year-old's smile.

"Nah, I'm good. Thank you for your hospitality. It was a real pleasure meeting you and your lovely wife."

'*Thank you George"*, said Ray.

They all shook hands and called it a night.

"Good night!" Gina yelled from the bedroom.

"Good night!" called out Tony and George simultaneously.

****

After getting into the car with Tony, George started throwing his fists up in the air.

"Whew, woah, oh yeah baby!" shouted George.

Both men started laughing.

"I told you to be careful what you wished for, right? Didn't I tell you?" asked Tony.

George looked over at Tony, and in excitement hugged him.

"Shit Tone, I feel like I've known you all of my life. You're the brother I've always wanted, but my mom never gave me."

"Thanks buddy."

They left the gated community and entered the highway, the music in the yellow beast thumping loudly. Tony's rested his head against the window of the car. As the car zoomed onward, Tony's eyes followed the objects that seemed to speed past the window. His eyes followed the "exit" sign that lead to his home as it disappeared into the distance. Tony picked up his head and looked over at George.

"Yo bro you missed the exit."

"Nah I didn't the night ain't over yet. There is still one more thing."

"George, I've had enough for tonight. I need a bed."

"Gimme ten minutes Tone."

"But where are we going?"

'To the West Side bro, relax, sit back,, and I'll wake you when we get there."

Ten minutes later, George shook Tony awake..

"Tone, Tone, wake up Tone."

"Yeah, yeah. Damn nigga, it's daylight out. What time is it?"

"It's 6:15 a.m."

"Where are we?"

"Come on."

The car was positioned in front of three car doors. It was a three-car garage behind two brick houses. George got out and Tony followed. The usual 6:30 a.m. spring silence ensued. Hardly any traffic could be heard. George gave Tony a little box with a button on it.

"Happy birthday my brother. Just press the button."

Tony pressed the button and up came the garage door to reveal a Porsche 911 in white. It was exactly the same as George's. Tony's mouth and eyes opened wide in disbelief. George threw him the key.

"Be careful what you wish for buddy", George said.

Tony grabbed him and hugged him.

"Thank you man."

"She's yours Tony-clean, clear, and legal. Go ahead, take it, I'll see you tomorrow."

Tony got in the car and smiled as he watched George reverse up the driveway and disappear. Tony grabbed the steering wheel and admired the interior of his new Porsche. Every ounce of sleep that he had had disappeared. Tony was pumped—he finally had his own white beast. He turned on the ignition, and she purred like a kitten. Tony put the car in first gear and re-entered the world.

****

Ring Ring Ring

"Hello?" asked Tony.

Torn

"Yo?"

"Who's this?"

"Me, George."

"Hey, what's up buddy?"

"Did I wake you? Let me guess, with all the excitement you couldn't sleep."

"Oh yeah man. Hey thanks again man for the…"

"No, no buddy, thanks for the porno experience last night bro. That was priceless."

'Oh bro, that was crazy wasn't it? Imagine how I felt when that shit happened to me."

"Hey come on man, breakfast on me at J.P's in an hour. I'll see you there."

'Okay."

One Hour Later

Tony only put in three hours of sleep, but the excitement of getting behind the wheel overcame everything. He was high on life.

Tony pulled into J.P.'s and decided to wait for George in the car. Ten minutes later the yellow beast pulled into the parking lot. George was not alone. Tony got out of his car and approached George's car. Both of the yellow beast's yellow doors opened. George got out, and from the passenger's side emerged the cutest five-year-old boy.

"Ethan come here. This is Tony, daddy's very good friend."

Evan looked at Tony from head to toe with the brightest green eyes, and stuck out his little hand. Tony shook it, *'Nice to meet you buddy. Wow, you're gonna be a real lady-killer when you grow up. Beautiful kid George, God bless him.'*

"Thanks bro."

Ethan seemed to be really friendly and attached. He immediately grabbed Tony's hand followed by his followed by his father's and started swinging himself from them. Tony and George walked into J.P's kid in tow. The 'ooohs" and "aaahs" came from the waitresses who were expressing how beautiful the child was. The waitress station was real busy within all the comments that were being made.

"Oh my God, look they adopted a little boy. That's so beautiful", said Madeline.

"Ah, I knew they were gay", said a waitress named Arlette.

"Oh just look at that beautiful picture. They're the perfect gay couple", said Nancy.

"Yeah, they should be gay couple of the year", whispered Kyle.

"Que lindo my God", said Kristina.

Tony, George and Ethan took a booth and Kristina appeared.

"Hi George, hi Tony. And who's this handsome little devil?"

"This is Ethan," said George. "He's five years old, say hi Ethan"

"Hi."

"Hi Ethan, Are you hungry Ethan?" asked Kristina

"Yes", replied the little boy.

Torn

"How about a hamburger with French fries?"

"Hmm, yes", said Ethan

"Okay, coming right up. And you guys the regular, right?"

"Yes", they said in unison.

She wrote down the orders and walked away.

"I'm gonna do it today bro" said Tony.

"Do what?" asked George.

"Hook Kristina."

"Yeah?" asked George excitedly.

"I wanna see how you do this", said George.

Kristina returned with the food and set it down on the table.

"If you need anything else, just flag me down."

"Okay", said George.

Kristina was about to walk away when Tony discreetly motioned to her that she had something on her nose. She panicked, covered her nose, and walked away in embarrassment. George stared at Tony.

"What the hell was that?" asked George.

"Easy buddy", said Tony, *"I'm just breaking down barriers and evening the playing field."*

"What do you mean?"

"Well you see, these pretty good looking girls think they're so

beautiful that they sit a little higher than everyone else. So what I do is make them realize otherwise by embarrassing them a little. This will drive them to impress you a little more, to make up for that flaw you noticed in them. Even if they're perfect, you need to create a flaw where it doesn't exist. Kristina didn't have anything on her nose, but I made her think she did, and I bet now she won't seem so conceited. You'll see now when she comes back. She'll act differently, or send someone else instead."

George looked at Tony with suspicion.

"Hmmm, I want to see how this plays out", said George.

"Okay, watch this."

Tony waved over at Kristina who was standing at the waitress station with the other waitresses. She held up her hand in a "hold on" motion.

"Watch this George."

Three minutes later, one of the other waitresses showed up.

"Hi guys. Kristina is a little tied up at the moment."

Tony looked over at George who was smiling in amazement.

"We'll take the check thank you."

"You're good", said George.

Tony took a napkin and wrote on it.

"Kristina, here's a fifty-dollar tip for your service. Please call me. I have a business proposition for you. 917-883-4822 – Tony."

"Here, can you please give this to Kristina?"

"Sure", said the waitress.

"Thank you."

They cleaned up little Ethan and got ready to leave. The waitress returned and handed Tony a napkin. George looked at Tony and as Tony opened the napkin, he smiled. The napkin read:

"Sorry Tony, I will not take your number because I'm not in the habit of calling the customers. What I will do is give you my number, and if you want to call me—you can. 917-555-7700. Kristina."

Tony and George looked at each other and gave each other a high five. Tony grabbed little Ethan and hugged him.

"Woo hoo! I love you little man!" Tony yelled.

RING RING RING

"Hello? Yeah. No I can't really talk right now bro. I'll call you back in five minutes", said George.

"Is everything okay?" asked Tony.

"Yeah, yeah everything's cool. Just business I need to tend to. I'll call you tonight, okay? Gotta go."

"Yeah, okay", replied Tony.

Tony helped Ethan into the car and strapped him in. George started to pull away from the lot and lowered his window.

"Congrats on the number!" George shouted as he pulled out of the parking lot.

****

Tony turned to get in his car. As he pulled on the door handle, he looked up at the restaurant window and immediately ducked. Tony hit the floor. Slowly, he crept up, opened his car door, and slid into the driver's seat. He put on a baseball cap and shades to disguise himself. He started the car and left the parking lot.

Tony circled the block and stopped two cars before reaching J.P.'s. He sat there and watched her argue with what appeared to be her significant other. Hands were waving and fingers were being pointed. The argument seemed to be pretty intense. After about forty-five minutes, she got up and walked away from the table. The other person got up and disappeared. Tony spotted her in the parking lot as she approached her car. She turned and leaned on the passenger's side door with her arms crossed. Tony spotted the driver approaching her.

The argument seemed to flare up again, with finger pointing in faces. After awhile, they both finally got into the car. The car screeched in reverse and pulled out. Tony put the gear in first and closely followed. The driver was very aggressive. At every light they stopped at, the hands came up and the argument commenced. After the fifth light, the driver placed a palm on the girl's face, and slammed her head against the door window. The door immediately opened and she stormed out of the car. She walked back towards Tony's car and the driver just drove off without thinking twice.

Tony sat there and pondered whether he should help her or just mind his own business. Tony thought it was fate. He wasn't just going to let it go. Tony waited for her to reach his car before making his move, but before he could do anything, Tony was startled when the car behind him blew his horn. Tony drove forward and passed her, but kept an eye on her through his rear view mirror. He then popped a U-Turn and slowly drove back up, admiring her posterior. She was a thoroughbred. Tony pulled up beside her and rolled down his window.

"Hey beautiful, do you want a ride?"

"No."

She didn't even look his way. She just kept on walking.

Torn

"Look we know each other. I just want to make sure you get home okay."

"I'm fine, and people I know are not stalkers—which you clearly are."

She still had not turned his way. Tony flipped open his phone and searched through the directory.

"917-415-0127 – Inez", he shouted.

Inez swung her head around and stared at Tony, trying to remember his face. She looked beautifully sad—enough to break Tony's heart. He got out of the car, walked around the front, and stood in front of her as she wept like a lost little girl. He held both of her hands and looked into her glazed, almond-shaped eyes.

"It's me Tony. We met at Mystiques not long ago."

Tears flooded down her cheeks. She looked at Tony and finally remembered. As she did, she wrapped her arms around his waist. Tony wrapped his arms around her as if he was shielding her from all harm. She felt safe in his arms. She knew it, and showed it. Tony escorted Inez to his car and as he walked around the front of the car, he looked at her through the windshield, and their eyes locked. Without a single word, they both felt the passion in each other's eyes. He got in and shut the door.

"You okay?"

Tony knew she wasn't, so he just took off instead of waiting for her to answer. He got onto the highway and just drove on with no destination.

"I don't want to go home", she said. "She'll be waiting for me at home."

Tony continued to drive in silence for what seemed to be about an

77

hour. He then pulled off an exit and entered what seemed to be and abandoned gas station. Tony shut the engine and adjusted himself to face her.

"Talk to me sweetheart. What's wrong?"

"She's such a jealous bitch, but when she gets caught she wants to try and flip it and beat the shit out of me."

"So you caught her with someone?"

"She left her cell phone at home. She went to the supermarket and the phone rang. Since we both bought our cell phones together, they're identical. I thought it was mine and I picked it up. The voice at the other end said, "I had a wonderful time last night Lilly." When I asked who it was, I guess the person on the other end of the line realized that I wasn't who she thought I was and hung up. Just to be sure, I picked up the house phone and dialed her number-and her phone rang again. When she got home, I approached her about the matter and she flipped out on me. She thought that I had purposely picked up her phone. She started screaming and suggested we go eat. I went with her to that restaurant because I'd had enough and planned to part with her."

"I see. Do you really want to break up with her?"

"Yes, you saw how jealous she got when she saw me talking to you at the club."

"How did you end up with that girl?" Tony asked.

"Well I didn't always like women Tony. I love men. She was the first woman I was with. She was a very good friend and the guy I had at the time used to hit me too. Every time he would beat me, she was always there with open arms when I needed her. I was vulnerable and she took advantage of that. She turned me out."

"So she turned you out just to do the same thing that your ex was

doing, huh?"

Inez began sobbing intensely. Tony grabbed her hands and kissed them.

"Hey, hey, hey, come on don't do this. Don't cry baby. You're too pretty to be crying."

"Gee shit, look at me. You must think I'm a freakin' nutcase."

"Look everyone's got a past, an issue, and off-the-wall ex partner, but as long as all that crap stays in the past and doesn't spill into the future, then you should be okay. I can't sit here and judge you because I have my own issues and off-the-wall situation, but I leave them where they belong – in the past. You are an extremely beautiful woman, and I can't even fathom you getting involved with such destructive and abusive people. But if you really want to leave this chick, just let me know and I'll do everything in my power to help you."

Inez looked at Tony and squeezed his hand. He saw her attempt to come toward him. He held his composure. She came closer and closer until she was just about an inch from his lips. She looked deeply into his eyes and he looked into hers. He felt her intense breaths through her nostrils. Tony looked at her lips and then up at her eyes. His subconscious wanted to rip through his body and devour Inez. He held off until she made her final move. She unleashed her tongue and it gently glided over his lips. He was content with just looking at her. That's how beautiful she was. Inez pulled her tongue back in her mouth and stared at him as if to say "your turn". Tony stuck his tongue out slowly and gently basted her lips with his tongue, traced the outline - leaving behind a trail of wet glaze.

Tony opened his eyes only to find that hers were closed. He grabbed her neck, just under the back of her head and guided her to join his lips. As his lips melded with hers, she melted all over him. She kept making small, pleasure moans and sighs. Although Tony knew she was okay, he kept being attentive.

"Are you okay?" he whispered.

"Hmm..never better."

She raised her face to join his lips and they kissed passionately until it was dark outside.

"It's getting late. You mind if we start heading back?" she asked.

"Of course, sure, where are we going?"

"Just take me to my mom's house. Lucern and Country Club Rd."

Tony started up the car and headed back.

"So you have no plans of going back home?"

"Not for some time. I'll probably go in while she's at work and move my stuff to my mom's house."

"Well if you need any help just let me know."

"Thank you", she said.

Inez settled in her seat, and after all the tears and exhaustion of the day she passed out. Tony gently reclined her chair and kept driving. He kept looking to the right, at her beautiful face while she slept. She looked like a little angel. Tony thought to himself as he drove, "When I said I knew she would be mine, I had no idea it would come in this form. Things happen in the most unexpected ways."

Tony drove in silence, staring at the black pavement and white lines zoom past him. His thoughts were driving him crazy. All of a sudden, flashes and thoughts of Kristina came to him. He turned to look at Inez. She was sound asleep. He turned his attention to the road again and thought of the possibilities or disasters of the road he was

Torn

attempting to go through.

"Two women as beautiful as they are and I could possibly have both, hmmm?" he thought to himself. Tony was interrupted by his vibrating phone.

"Hello?"

"Tony?"

"It's me Ray."

"Big Ray, what's up? How's your beautiful wife?'

"She's great, thanks. Hey man, how's this guy George? Is he good? I mean is he a stand-up guy? Do you trust him?"

"Hey, why do you ask?"

"Nah, nothing, just wanted to know—that's all bro. No big deal."

"On a personal level he's good people. He's shown me nothing but brotherly love. He wants to open a club with me. We're just waiting for the right place to become available, ya know. As far as business is concerned, ours hasn't taken off, but I have no doubt that he'll be stand up about it. *Does that make sense?"*

"Yeah, Tone thanks. I'm good. Hey listen – my wife says she wants to know when you can come over and play."

Tony let out a chuckle.

"I don't know buddy. I just passed my Real Estate Broker's exam and I'm looking to open up an office soon, so I'm going to be pretty tied up for a while. But as soon as I straighten everything out, we'll hook up and have a grand opening party. What do you think?"

"Tone that sounds like a plan. Just let me know the day and time,

81

and congrats on passing that test."

"Thanks bro, I'll see you soon."

"Okay bro, later."

Tony pulled up to Lucern and Country Club Rd. and stopped. Inez was out like a light. Tony gently moved a few strands of hair away from her forehead to reveal her angelic face. He gently caressed her supple face with the backside of his hand.

"Pssst, pssst, baby we're here."

She moaned and turned around into a fetal position, grabbed his arm, and put it around her. She moaned again as if she didn't want to leave.

"Baby, you're here."

"Hmmm, baby I don't want to leave", she said.

Tony smiled. He knew he had her. He put his face next to hers and kissed her ears and cheeks. He gave her little pecks of passion, kissing her ever so slightly – just barely touching her skin. Her goosebumps confirmed he was on the right track. She suddenly turned and faced him.

"I wish you would stay with me tonight."

"Yeah, that would be nice sweetie, but this is your mom's house and I don't want to meet your mom under these circumstances. I also have business early tomorrow."

She looked into his eyes.

"Thank you", she said.

"For what?"

Torn

"For listening for not judging me, and for being a gentleman."

She then plastered her succulent, rich, and luscious lips on his and kissed him.

"Thanks again", she said.

She opened the car door, got out, shut it and pranced into her mother's house.

Tony gripped the steering wheel and smiled. He felt incredibly supercharged, attractive, rich, and cocky. He couldn't put a finger on exactly what it was that made him feel that way, but he loved it. The goal he set at the club had materialized in this form. He revved the engine twice and took off. He approached the stop light at Country Club Rd. and Bruckner Blvd. As he waited for the light to change, a swirl of emotions entered him. *His heartbeat was hard, and his thoughts were on Inez.*

****

"My God", he thought, "I'm thirty-one years old and I've never felt this feeling." His heart wanted to leap out of his chest. The thumps were almost audible. His phone rang.

"Hello?"

"Hi, I was just thinking about you. I can't get you off of my mind Tony", said Inez.

"Really?"

"Really", she said.

"Hmmm."

"Where are you right now?"

83

"At the light on Country Club Rd."

Suddenly sounds of screeching tires diverted Tony's attention to his rear view mirror, where he saw a pair of headlights zooming toward him.

"oh shit, what the fuck!" said Tony
"what happened?"

Tony was paralyzed by what he was anticipating. It came in slow motion. Tony braced his steering wheel and winced as he heard every crack from the smash. He was thrown forward by the impact. His phone smashed against the windshield causing the battery to disengage.

"Hello, Hello? Tony are you there?"

The call went dead.

"What the fuck? My fucking car!"

That was all Tony could think about. He swung the door open and crept out of the car. He limped toward the rear of the car to assess the damage. Drips of blood flowed down his nose and into his mouth, staining his teeth. Lying on the floor were shards of glass that came from the smashed rear tail-lights.

"Fuck!"

He turned to the car and it looked familiar. He approached the car and saw the driver bent over the steering wheel. He opened the door and pulled the driver back. Her face was covered in blood.

"Fuck lady! What the fuck is wrong with you?"

He struggled to contain his anger. The rear of his dream car was smashed to pieces. The woman was motionless. He grabbed her, carried her to the passenger seat of his car, and secured her. He tried to hurry back to her car to see if he could get some information as to who she was. He grabbed her keys from the ignition and opened her trunk.

"What the fuck is this shit?"

There lay a box with four chicken claws tied together, a jar with slimy liquid, an assortment of candles, and assortment of colored beaded necklaces, and a box with two black pigeons.

"This crazy bitch", he murmured.

He shut the door of the trunk, got into his car, and headed over to Jacobi Hospital. On his way there, he kept looking at the woman, wondering what the hell could all that shit in the trunk have been. He grabbed her face and turned it toward him. She was out cold.

"What a shame, so pretty and so fucked up", he whispered.

He arrived at the hospital and entered through the E.R's glass sliding doors with her draped in his arms. His bloody face and her motionless body garnered the attention of the nearby staff that responded immediately. They took her from him and disappeared. Thirty minutes later he was out the door. He looked at the rear of his white beast and shook his head in anguish.

Tony went back to Country Club Rd. went into the woman's car and started looking around for anything that would give him an indication of who this woman was. He looked and looked. Finally, he found a small purse up under the passenger seat rug. The car's impact sent the purse flying under the dashboard—and pushing it under the rug. He zipped open the purse and fumbled through it – a cell phone, lipstick, hairpins, a lighter, and cigarettes. He pulled out the cell phone and flipped it open. The LCD display read "Lilly's Phone". The phone was equipped with a camera. He accessed the camera function to flip through the photos.

"What the fuck? Photos of my car?"

As he flipped through the phone, he saw photos of his car, of him dropping Inez off an hour earlier, and of him kissing Inez. Then he saw a picture of Inez at her house naked, and finally a picture of the woman kissing Inez.

"Fuck!"

Tony left the car, took the cell phone, and left. On his way home, he decided to call Inez from Lilly's phone since his was smashed from the accident.

RING RING

"Listen, do me a favor. Lose my number. I don't care for your jealous bouts. I'll have all my shit out of the apartment this week. Don't call me anymore." CLICK

Inez hung up. Tony called back.

"I told you not to call me anymore. What is it you don't…"

"Hey, hey, it's me Tony."

"Who?"

"Tony."

"What are you doing? What happened? It's been over two hours since the call fell through, and Why are you calling me from Lilly's phone?"

"Look Inez, Your crazy bitch ex- girlfriend has been watching us all night. *She's taken picture of us, parked in front of your mom's house spying—"*

"How do you know all this?"

"Well because the bitch rammed my car-doing 60 mph, busted my

nose, smashed my cell phone, and wrecked her own car in the process. I left her car on Country Club Rd. I also rushed her to Jacobi Hospital."

"What?" she exclaimed in confusion.

"That's right—that crazy bitch tried to kill me. I was at the light talking to you when I took notice of the screeching tires. I looked up and it was too late."

"Oh my God Tony. I'm sorry! I'll pay for the damages to your car. I'm sorry!"

"Hey, don't worry about it. I'll take care of it. I'm going home to rest. I'll bring you this phone tomorrow. See what you can do about her car. It's still there. The keys are under the mat."

Inez was at a loss for words. She became silent on the phone.

"Hello? You still there?"

"Yes" she said hesitantly. *"I feel so horrible. For the first time in my life I meet someone who is so different, and because you tried to help me—this happened to you. I'm so sorry."*

"Babe, I'll take care of it. Don't stress it, okay?"

"Alright" she said.

"Good night Inez."

"Good night."

****

Tony entered his apartment, grabbed the house phone, and called George.

RING RING

"Hello?"

"George? It's me Tone."

"What's up Tone? Can't sleep?"

"Bro you don't know what happened to me."

"What happened? You okay? Stay there, I'll be right over."

Twenty minutes later, the buzzer rang. Tony buzzed George in.

'Whoa! Bro, who did this to your face? What happened? Is the nose broken?"

"Nah, nah. I'm alright man—just some scratches."

"Scratches? Shiiiit, I'll fuck somebody up. Do you need something or do you want to get these guys yourself?"

"Nah bro, I'm straight but my baby looks worse."

Tony looked at George and winced in pain.

"The car?" asked George.

Tony nodded.

"Yup."

"Well let's see the damage."

They went out back and stood three feet from the rear of the car. They both folded their arms and tilted their heads. After a few minutes of silence, they stared at each other simultaneously.

"Well? What do you think?" asked Tony.

"Hmmmm, lucky for you—I have those parts."

"Okay, I guess my next question is, How much is this gonna cost me?"

"Don't worry about it. I'll pick up the car tomorrow and I'll get it done. Just tell me what happened."

After the explanation George shook his head in disappointment. He started laughing and jokingly said,

"You see, if you would've tried to get them both at the same time-none of this shit would've happened."

They shared the laugh and as George made his way out he said,

"Come with me, I have another phone in my car. You can have it."

He gave Tony the phone.

"Thanks George. I'll have it up and running by tomorrow. I'll call you when it's up so you can pick up the car.'

"Okay" said George.

****

By 10 a.m. the next morning, Tony called George to come pick up the car. The yellow beast rounded the corner and pulled up next to Tony who was waiting outside.

"It'll be easier if you just follow me bro."

"Okay" said Tony.

Tony followed George for thirty minutes toward the Northeast Bronx.

They arrived at a driveway between a brick, two-story home and a Rite Aid pharmacy. They drove down the driveway and parked. Both men got out of their respective cars and entered the two-car garage. The garage went back about one hundred feet.

"Go get your car and pull it in here."

Tony drove in and saw two more Porches, both 911's. Just behind them was a stockpile of Porches parts. Hanging on the walls were fenders, hoods, doors, bumpers, and miscellaneous parts. Tony got out of his car and went towards the red 911 that was there.

'Yo, who's is this?"

"Ah, just a car that my partner stole from FBI headquarters."

"FBI headquarters?" Tony laughed. *"Nah for real man who owns this?"*

"My partner stole it from FBI headquarters."

Tony looked at George and he was not laughing. He had a penetrating look on his face.

"You see that blue jacket on the seat there. Pick it up and look at it."

Tony picked up the jacket. Sprawled on the back of the jacket were the letters FBI in big, bold, and yellow letters.

"Look in the trunk" said George.

Tony opened the trunk and saw two bullet-proof vests. He dropped the trunk lid and jumped back.

"These fucking cars are stolen!" he yelled.

"Haven't I been tryin' to tell you that for the past three minutes."

"Is my car stolen?"

"No buddy, I owned three of them. Yours was one of mine."

"Did you steal them?"

"No, I didn't. My partner Vlad did. I only sell the parts. My partner Vlad, the technician, does everything. I just broker the deals."

"So you're selling stolen parts and dealing stolen cars?" asked Tony.

"Tony, Tony, I'm a businessman. So, if the technician wants me to put him in touch with someone who's looking for a particular part or car, what's the harm in passing along a number? He deals directly with the guy and when the deal is done he gives me $500 per head."

"Hmmmm" said Tony.

Tony took it all in. He had never been exposed to any of that element. Tony felt a thrill. He didn't want to admit it. Although he thought his own car wasn't legit, he didn't want to jump the gun just yet.

"When do you think she'll be ready?"

George gave the car a once over.

"Hmmm, three days. C'mon let me take you home."

"Okay, let's go" said Tony.

They got onto the highway.

"Hey I think I'm going to open my real estate office next month."

"Yeah?"

"Yeah bro. I'm psyched about it bro."

"Man Tone, you're all over the place. Stripper, personal trainer, promoter, real estate broker, what else?"

Tony stood in silence looking out of the window.

"You okay buddy?" asked George.

"Look I come from the gutter man. My mom was on welfare. Then, when I was old enough, I had to go on welfare too. I always wondered why I wasn't born with a silver spoon in my mouth. So I figured if I could get certified in everything under the sun, then I'd always be in a position to make money. I'll never go back to being on welfare. Next month I will open up my real estate office and consider myself a success."

George stood quiet. Tony looked at him wondering if he said something wrong. All of a sudden, George yelled.

"Yeah baby! Hey I'm looking to buy a house, can I be your first customer?"

Tony laughed and George joined him.

"I'm serious."

'Bro, let me open up shop first."

"Nah bro, all jokes aside, what can I do to contribute?"

"Well I would like to throw a nice grand opening party. Call John at J.P.'s and tell him I want them to cater the party and Kristina to be the head waitress."

"Consider it done. What else?"

"I don't know. We've got a month to figure it out. I still have to secure a location. I saw a place up in Throggs Neck that I really like. I'm going to try to get it. When I do, I'll give you the details."

Torn

****

Jacobi Hospital

"Hi, I'm here to see a patient."

"Name please."

"Lillian Lopez."

"Let's see. Hmmm, okay - 7 South. That's on the seventh floor, Room 721. Take the second elevator on your right."

"Thank you."

She entered the elevator and arrived.

"716, 718, 720. Maybe it's the other side" she said to herself.

"Ah, 721."

She walked into the room and saw Lilly there facing the window.

"Hey?"

Lilly looked over from the window and smiled.

"Hi baby. I didn't expect to see you here. How did you know I was here?"

"Well I wasn't planning on coming, and the guy you tried to hurt, who possibly saved your life, told me you were here. What happened, and why did you do that?"

"What guy? What are you talking—"

"Ay Lilly! Stop it alright? Stop being such a fuckin' liar! I know

93

everything!"

"Wait, wait, wait Inez. Look, the truth is that I went to your mom's house to try to make it right between us and there was no one home. I decided to wait down the block until someone got home and then I saw a car pull up and drop you off. I saw you guys kissing and hugging, and it infuriated me. Last I remember, he was at a light and then I blacked out."

"Blacked out, huh?"

"Inez I'm sorry baby. I didn't mean for us to fight the way we did. I want to start fresh. Inez I love you so much that—"

"No, no, no Lilly. When you "blacked out", you smashed Tony's car and for what? Do you think—"

"Who the fuck is Tony?!"

"Shut up!" Inez screamed. "Let me fuckin' finish. Do you think that's gonna make me want you? Oh, and you need to thank your lucky ass that he's the real man that he is, because if you would've smashed my car like that, I would have let you bleed to death! If you didn't die, I would've sued your ass! You're fuckin' lucky he brought you here!"

"Inez I'm sorry. I don't want to lose you!"

"Lilly, I think it's a little too late for that bullshit. I've caught you countless times and you act so blasé about it, like you don't give a shit. Now I really like this guy, and if you love me like you say you do, you'll be happy for me in knowing that I'm happy seeing this guy."

"Happy? Why the hell would I be happy for you when you want to be with someone else? If you and him think that I'm just gonna roll over like a beat dog, you've got another thing coming. I'm gonna keep trying. I'm no quitter."

"Lilly, it's over. Your car is at Country Club Rd. Here are your keys and Tony's bringing me your phone tomorrow. When he does, I'll return it. Bye."

"Inez?!"

Inez turned around and walked out of the room as she wiped the tears off her cheeks.

"Inez, Inez, Inez!" Lilly yelled, but there was no answer. Inez was gone.

****

RING RING

"Hello?"

"Kristina, please."

"Speaking, who's this?"

"Hi Kristina, it's me George. We eat at the restaurant. I go with Tony a couple of times a week?"

"Yeah, yeah, how's Tony?"

"He's good thanks. That's why I'm calling. I want your restaurant to cater a party that I want to throw for him and I want you to be the head waitress. It will be on Feb. 15th and bring a little cake. My birthday falls on Valentine's day, but the 15th will do."

"Okay, I need the address and what it is you want on the menu."

"Okay, I'll go there personally and give it to you. I'll see you tonight at J.P.'s. "

"Okay."

****

Lilly was discharged from the hospital and immediately jumped on the 6 train, and headed for Manhattan. Forty minutes later, she got off at the 166th street station and entered the streets of Harlem. She headed toward Park Avenue and turned to 114th street. On the corner stood a red brownstone building. Lily went up the three steps and rang the buzzer. The buzzer rang out and she entered the gloomy urine-scented corridor. She headed toward the rear door. As she approached the door, the smell of urine disappeared and the smell of incense emerged from beneath the door. African drum sounds now took a hold of her ears as they echoed through the hallways. She knocked on the door. As the door opened, a thick cloud of incense smoke escaped the apartment and the drumbeat sound became clearer and louder.

"Entra mija" said Freddy, an effeminate Santeria godfather wearing all white-inlcuding a white hat, and multicolored necklaces.

"Hi padrino."

"I heard about your accident. Let's see if we can make things better."

"I need help padrino."

"I know mami, I know, come with me."

Lilly followed Freddy through a maze of smoke and drums. The sound became more and more pronounced with every step, reverberating through the walls. It seemed to be coming from one the ritual rooms down the hall.

"Come sit here mija."

Lilly sat behind a small table flanked by a red tablecloth. On the table sat a bowl of water with a crucifix and half a burnt cigar. Lilly looked around the room. She saw an altar with thirteen different ceramic statues, all representing different saints. Before the saints were bowls of water, money, fruits, candy, corn on the cob, and other sweets that were spiritually offered to them by visitors, in an attempt to sweeten their own lives. Several boxes lay on the floor. In them were chicken, doves, and pigeons.

"Mija, were you able to do what I told you?"

"No Freddy. I got into the accident and the stuff is still in the trunk."

"Aye, aye, aye, que paso? What happened?"

"I crashed into that car and ended up in the hospital. From what I heard, he was the one who brought me into the hospital."

"Are you sure you want to do this to this man who possibly saved your life?"

"Yeah, fuck it. Just get him out of my way. Put him in jail and do something with her so that I can come to her rescue. I don't know, put her in the hospital or something – nothing serious, but enough to keep her in there a couple of days. He can't be that perfect. He's gotta be hiding something."

"Okay."

Freddy lit a candle and grabbed both her hands. He bowed his head and started reciting and chanting spiritual songs – calling on all of his gods. He then sat up and started speaking in a deep, demonic voice. Lilly sat back startled but attentive.

"This man has a lot of love for this woman. He loves women. Too strong, too fast, too much. This man is not the man he portraying himself to be. He has others. But they are blinded by his charming ways. Break the trance he has them in and she will be yours."

Antonio Torres

Suddenly Freddy violently slumped over the table, smashing it with his forehead. Lilly jumped back.

"My God padrino, you okay?" asked with a concerned expression on her face.

"Ay mija, what happened?"

"I don't know. Some other voice said some things, then you smashed the table with your head."

"Was it a he or a she?"

"It was a man with a deep voice."

"What did he say?"

"He said that this guy had others and that because he was so charming they were blinded and couldn't see it."

"Well now we know how to handle this. You must do every thing I say and give it time to work. It could be six days, six weeks, or six months, but it will work. First, you will got to the Botanica and buy cinnamon extract, Benzoin, anise extract, Holy Water, Ground yam, sandlewood, apple blossom extract, rosemary, lemon juice, and a slug or a live snail, three different kinds of mercury, moonshine liquor, and some rum. Get petals from the following flowers: Forget me nots, pansies, Roses, and Lillies. Get the following herbs: Rue, mimosa, yamao, parami, amansa, guapo and "duermete puta". Place all of these into a one gallon jug, add to that "High Join the Conqueror" root and three drops of your urine to the mix, plus three drops of urine from a bitch in heat. You must do all of this on a Good Saturday of Easter Week. Say the "Prayer of the Lonely Soul" three times and leave the gallon by Elleguas Laye's altar for three days. The day you decide to use this with her, you will be irresistible, not only to her, but everyone else. So be careful. If you want to use my Elleguas Altar you can."

98

"Thank you padrino."

****

February 15th – The Grand Opening

Tony was stuck in traffic and the grand opening was set to start in fifteen minutes. Tony called George, unaware that George was already there.
"Hello George?"

"Yeah, where you at?"

"Bro, I'm stuck in traffic. Bumper to bumper shit!"

"Well try to hurry up. I'm on my way" said George.

"Okay, I'll see you there bro."

Tony called Inez to invite her to the party.

RING

"Hello beautiful."

"Hiii! How are you? Listen, I want to apologize for what happened a couple of weeks ago. I called you a couple of times and you never returned my calls."

"No need to apologize sweetheart. My nose is still in one piece, and as far as returning your call goes, I want to apologize. *I've been really busy trying to open my business-which leads me to my next question. What are you doing tonight?"*

"Nothing, why?"

"Would you like to come to my grand opening party?"

99

"Of course I would love to come."

"Well I'm on my way there. I'll call you back to give you the address. Do you have a ride?"

"Yeah, give me about an hour" she said.

"Okay, I'll see you there."

Tony arrived and pulled into the parking spot. He got out. When he tried to open the locks, they were already open. He stepped inside. It was dark, no noise, no light, nothing. He stepped back outside, wondering where everyone was. He called George.

RING RING

"Hello"

"Yo, it's me Tone. I'm here and there's no one here, and the door was open bro."

"Look I'm in traffic now. I'm one exit away. In the meantime start setting everything up."

"Okay bro."

"Later."

Tony pulled up parked and headed downstairs to the office . When he reached the bottom of the staircase, he flipped on the light switch.

"SURPRISE!!!" they all screamed.

There were over fifty people there. George was in the corner laughing. He was never in traffic. They were there all along. The food and liquor flowed freely. George came forward and behind him stood Kristina holding a tray of food. She handed Tony a glass of champagne.

Torn

"Congratulations Tony, enjoy."

"Thank you love."

Rick, Gina, Ray, Big Chris, and all the dancers were there. Kristina and the waitresses, Artie, and even people that Tony didn't know were there. Tony looked around and knew he had made it. He crawled out of the gutter. He looked at George and gave him a thumbs up. Gina approached Tony and leaned over to him.

"Are we playing tonight?"

Tony knew she was coked up and the drinking made it worse for her. Tony was turned off.

"I don't know Gina. I've had a long day and from what it looks like here, I'll be having a long night."

"And I can make it an even longer night" she said while smiling.

"I tell you what, I'll let Ray know okay?"

"Okay" she said. She smiled and kissed Tony on the lips. George walked over to Tony.

"You okay Tony?"

"Yeah I'm good. That Gina is something, huh?"

"Yeah bro, she's hot."

"Oh shit George!"

"What?"

"I just remembered, Inez is on her way here."

"So?"

101

Antonio Torres

"So Kristina's here."

"Who invited Inez?" asked George.

"I did."

"But why Tone?"

"Uhh, because she's beautiful. I like her. Uhhh, let's see—should I keep going?"

"But what about Kristina?" asked George.

"How the hell was I supposed to know Kristina was going to be here when you hid everything from me?"

"Oh well, surprise!" George laughed. *"Look Tone, just play it cool, don't attach yourself when she comes."*

"It's been three hours and she's not here yet, so maybe that's good."

"Maybe not. What if she got into an accident or something?"

Tony turned around and headed upstairs towards the exit. He called Inez. The voice mail came on.

"Hey Inez. It's Tony. I spoke to you three hours ago and you're still not here. Call me. Let me know you're okay. Bye."

Tony joined the party again.

"Is she coming?" asked George.

"I got her voicemail."

"Bro, just enjoy yourself bro. If she comes-she comes, if not, fuck it."

"You're right bro, fuck it!"

102

Two hours later people started making their way out. The party was dwindling and Tony was exhausted.

"Hey Tone you coming? We're going to Ray's" said George.

Tony didn't want to go over there. He knew George was going and he was happy for him, after all, he deserved it. Putting together a party like this was not an easy task.

"Nah man I'm tired, but enjoy it brother."

They hugged each other and George handed Tony an envelope.

"This is for the waitress staff. Divide it the way you want it."

"Thanks bro."

Everyone was gone except the waitress staff. Tony sat there and watched at the waitress staff cleaned up. He watched as Kristina made her fluid movements. She was poetry in motion.

"Kristina, can I speak to you?"

"Sure."

She walked over to Tony.

"Hey, tell your girls to go home. I'll clean up the rest. Tell them you'll pay them tomorrow. I'll give you the money tonight, but I'd like to speak to you alone."

"Okay."

As the girls made their way out they waved good night. Tony waved back and they were gone. Tony was a little uncomfortable with the idea that Inez might show up.

"Hey you can put that down and come sit over here." He pointed at

the seat beside him.

"First of all this is yours."

Tony handed Kristina the envelope. She looked at him, grabbed the envelope, and looked away as if she didn't want to maintain eye contact.
"You are truly beautiful. Look at me."

He grabbed her chin and tilted her head up so that their eyes could meet. He stared into her eyes. Slowly he moved in closer and tilted his head to kiss her voluptuous lips.

"Whoa, whoa. Tony wait, how could you do this?"

"Do what? If you have a boyfriend, or if I've offended you, I'm sorry."

"My boyfriend, no. But what about you?"

"No, I don't have a girlfriend."

" Not girlfriend - boyfriend" she said.

"Boyfriend!?" he asked surprisingly.

"Yeah, aren't you and George involved?"

"Involved! What the hell?!"

"Are you guys not lovers?"

"What? What's wrong with you? I'm a straight man. Why on earth would you?...."

"Look I'm sorry ok?! It's that you guys always come to the restaurant together. You guys have never brought in any girls, you both dress incredibly well, you tip well, you ask for fruity sangria

and you bring in this beautiful child holding both your hands, what the hell am I supposed to think? I'm not the only one either. Everyone at JP's thinks you guys are gay."

Tony started laughing. She looked at him and joined him in laughter.

"Wow, so tell me, how long have I been gay?" she looked at him, smiled and said, *"Honey, even our boss has an inclination that you swing the other way."*

"What?" Tony laughed. *"Oh my God are you serious? How can you just make those assumptions about people you don't even know? Ha! Wait till George hears this one."*

He turned to look at her.

"Well, Kristi now that you know I'm not gay why don't. . ."

Before Tony could finish his sentence, she was all over him-kissing and licking his lips to her hearts content.

She stopped suddenly and said *"Listen, I've been up on my feet all night and as much as I would like to continue to kiss you and devour you, I'm really feeling uncomfortable."*

"Why?"

"Well I would feel much better if I had a shower and a change of clothes."

"So my place or yours?" Tony asked.

"I live with my mom."

"Whoa, I guess It's gonna be my place."

He grabbed her hand and as they left, he flicked off the lights and locked the door.

****

"Can we stop by my house so I can pick up some clothes?"

"Sure."

Tony pulled up in front of a five-story walk up.

"Is your mom okay with you staying out?"

"Well, we'll find out tonight won't we?"

"Here, give her my number and tell her you'll be at my house and that she can reach you anytime tonight at that number."

She stared at Tony for a moment, sort of surprised by his offer.

Once they arrived at Tony's house, he immediately drew the bathtub full of hot steamy water and doused it with lavender oil.

"I drew the bath for you."

"Thank you, baby."

He directed her to the bathroom and dimmed the lights.

"If you need anything just holler ok?"

"Sure."

Tony stepped out of the bathroom and started to set the ambiance. He lit the scented candles and set the sound system to Luther Vandross's angelic tunes. He dimmed the lights and put a bottle of wine to chill. Tony looked around one last time to make sure everything was in order before he lit the fireplace. He walked to the bathroom. The door was slightly ajar, enough so that he saw her reflection in the mirror. She lay in the tub with her head tilted back, just relaxing. The heat from the trickling water started to fog the mirror.

Torn

"Hey you, are you ok?" he asked

"Hmmmmm, yeah," she moaned with a smile, *"you can come in if you want."*

He slowly opened the door and walked in. She smiled at him.

"I feel so relaxed, what's that smell?"

"Just some peach scented candles that I lit."

He sat at the edge of the tub. He grabbed the soap and started to rub her shoulders. She sat up to give him access to her entire back. He pressed down gently as he went down her back. She started moaning indicating to him that she loved it. He continued up the side of her neck, she moaned again then she threw her head back and her eyes met his. He looked at her lips and gently kissed them. He suckled her bottom lip and pulled away gently causing it to snap back. He continued to seduce her. She shook like a leaf out of nervousness.

Suddenly, she grabbed him and pulled him in causing the water to splash up and onto the floor. They continued to kiss passionately. She tried to pull his soaked shirt off with a sense of erotic urgency, but couldn't. He detached himself from her lips to pull the shirt off then engaged in the lip lock again. Then she stopped.

"What's the matter, are you ok?" he asked.

She stared at him in silence.

"Look, Kristi if you're uncomfortable we can just sit a while."

She broke the stare and shook her head, *"No, that's ok."*

There he was between her legs facing her cramped in the cast iron tub in the most knee busting uncomfortable position wearing soaked jeans and ruined shoes.

107

"Why don't you take those off?" she asked.

He smiled, *"Good Idea, I thought you'd never ask."*

He stood up, remained between her legs, and started to pull his pants off. She reached up and pulled them down the rest of the way. Her wet slippery hands caressed his Herculean Thighs. She continued to rub them up and down, while looking up and staring at him. His eyes were shut as he savored every moment.

"I never thought thigh rubbing could ever feel this good", he thought to himself.

She grabbed and gently massaged his balls, then grabbed his dick and lathered it until it grew. She ignored it and moved to his navel, lower abdomen, and into his belly button with her soapy fingers.

"Jesus Christ, I love this girl" he thought.

She went up to lather his chest and collarbone.

"Raise your arms", she whispered.

She dug deep into his armpits and scrubbed up and down his arms, right up to his wrist, then to his palms where their eyes and lips met once again.

"Turn on the shower and rinse off, I'll be waiting for you in your bedroom." she said softly. After a few minutes of rinsing he exited the shower. Tony made his way toward the bedroom leaving a trail of wet footprints behind. He looked into the bedroom and saw the low amber glow of the flickering candlelight. He walked in and saw her naked body through a sheer laced skintight dress. It looked dreamy to him. She wore open toed high-heeled shoes that laced up past her calves. She lay there propped up on her elbows just staring at him. He stood there dripping wet staring at her overly glossed lips.

She stared at him from head to toe watching as the drops of water fell from his hair, to his rippling chest, to his washboard abs. He walked over to the bed and one knee at a time he climbed onto the bed. He crawled up to her and placed his hand on her face, caressed it and said, *"You're so beautiful."*

She smiled, threw her arms around him, and hugged him for what seemed to be an eternity. They kissed and made love through the night. It was slow, passionate love making. It was not crazy jungle fucking, butt fucking, or monkey sex. It was typical missionary and doggy style but it was one of the most beautiful experiences he had ever had. Although his sex escapades in the past were exciting and one of a kind, he never felt with anyone what he felt that night with Kristina. It was bliss.

****

Tony felt an intense ray heating up his face. He squinted trying to open his eyes, but the light was blinding. The intense sunlight was blaring through the window, right into his face. He quietly crept off the bed and closed the drapes. The darkness brought relief to his face and eyes. He looked at Kristina. She was sound asleep.

"What a vision, so beautiful, so perfect" he thought.

He left the bedroom and mounted the Stairmaster butt naked, thinking and retracing the events that had occurred the night before.

"How can I be falling for this girl so soon? I mean these feelings that I'm feeling are so intense" he pondered, *"What am I fucking whipped?"*

Then the inexplicable happened. As he stepped and stepped thoughts of Inez started penetrating his mind who was equally as beautiful and seemed to be equally as perfect as Kristina.

"Damn it, why am I thinking of Inez?"

After 30 minutes he jumped off the machine, took a shower and headed to the kitchen where he started to make bacon and eggs, toasted butter rolls, and for dessert-a delicious strawberry almond butter pound cake topped with amaretto cookies and whipped cream.

He brought it into the bedroom, placed it on the nightstand and sat on the floor and watched as the scent of the food passed her nostrils. Her nose moved and her nostrils flared indicating that the scent was registering. She inhaled deeply and smiled. She opened her eyes slightly and looked at him.

"Wow what did I do to deserve this?"

"You don't need to do anything to deserve this. This is the way you should always be treated. Good morning beautiful"

He got up and gave her a kiss on the forehead.

"Hold that thought" she said.

She jumped up and ran to the bathroom. She returned with mint fresh breath and planted a kiss right on his lips.

"Hmmmmmm, this is delicious, who taught you how to cook?"

"Food Network," he replied.

She laughed *"Wow, God it's delicious"*

"Thank you, enjoy." He left her and went into the kitchen to clean up. He dug into his pocket to check his phone, 4 missed calls, 1 from George, 3 from Inez.

"Shit, Inez what could she want."

His heart thumped hard but he didn't understand why. He wasn't attached to any of them but he wanted to be. He wanted to call her, even if just to make sure she was okay, but he knew it would be the wrong thing to do so he withheld.

Torn

"That was delicious, thank you."

Startled, he jumped up, and the phone went crashing down into the floor sending the battery and phone in two different directions.
"Oh I'm sorry I didn't mean to scare you baby."

"Oh, no, no, no don't be silly. I've got butter fingers, I'm glad you liked your breakfast. It was my pleasure and like I said, you should never have to wake up and not have that at your bedside."

They embraced and kissed.

"Can you drop me off at work?"

"Sure you ready?"

"Gimme 5 minutes."

"OK." She headed to the bathroom to prep.

"Ok, I'm ready."

They left the apartment. He rounded the car and opened the door for her. She got in and shut the door. He ran around the front and got in and took off.

****

"Are you ok?" he asked

"Never better. I had a wonderful time last night. I had and felt feelings that I've never felt before. It was weird. I hardly know you that way, yet I feel totally safe with you."

"I'm glad I was able to make you feel that way. Still think I'm gay?"

She looked at him and started laughing.

111

"What was I thinking?" she said.

He pulled in front of J.P.s' and she looked at him.

"Thank you for a wonderful night."

"You're welcome have a great day at work."

They kissed and she made her way into the restaurant.

Tony stared as she walked away *"Come on baby look back, look back, look back"* he thought to himself.

She turned looked back and waved goodbye.
"Yes, baby!" he said as he waved back.

He drove away and picked up his cell phone. He speed dialed George.

RING RING

"Hello?"

"George?"

"Yo, whats up?"

"It's me Tony."

"What's up Tone? Called you at 2:30am last night, where were you?"

"Home why, what happened?"

"Nah nothing. After the party last night we went back to Ray's place and the party got a little crazy, but they didn't want to start until you showed up. So that's why I called you.

Torn

They're the ones who kept bugging me to call so you could come by."

"Oh, nah man I had a little party of my own bro."
"Oh yeah?"

"Yeah bro with our waitress"

"Noooooooooo, the waitress?!"

"Yup, bro it happened, I did it."

"So is she the one?"

"What are we in the fuckin Matrix? Nah it definitely felt very different, weird, some shit I've never felt before."

"Did Inez ever show up?"

"Nah, I checked my phone this morning and I had 3 missed calls from her."

"Did you call her back?"

"Nope, you're the first person I'm calling today."

"Nigga, call her and ask her why she didn't show up."

"Where are you?"

"I'm on my way home from Ray's."

"Now?!"

"Yeah, it was an all nighter when I left. Him and Gina were still at it."

"Daayyeemmm, that boy's gonna have a freakin heart attack."

113

"Yeah tell me about it. Hey, congrats on the opening."

"Thanks bro. Oh and thank you for the surprise party man, I really appreciate that."

"Nah bro don't worry about that, there'll be many more. How's the car running?"

"She's running great bro."

"Hey Tone I was serious about being your first customer."

"You were?"

"Yeah, bro "

"What type of house are you looking for?"

"I'm looking for an income producing property that I can live out of."

"Ok, I should have something coming in about a week or so over on St. Lawrence Ave."

"How much?"

"Don't know yet but I'll keep you posted."

"Ok, cool."

"Aiight, call you later."

He hung up and called Inez.

RING RING

"Hello?"

"Inez?"

"Tony?" she asked

"Yeah, hi, is everything ok?"

"Yeah, I'm so sorry about last night."

"No, it's ok I just wanted to make sure everything was ok, you know no accidents and all."

"No, no I'm safe, I'm sorry I should've called, will you let me make it up to you?"

"No, really. It's not necessary "

"Plleeeeeeeaaase?"

"Ok, you win."

"Good, come over tomorrow."

"Where?"

"To my house, come by about noon"

"Ok, I'll be there sweety, bye"

"Bye."

Tony was excited to the point of disbelief. He was fortunate enough to know two beautiful women the way he was getting to know them.

****

12 p.m. the next day

Ring Ring

"Hello?"

"Hey it's me, Tony."

"Hi."

"I'm downstairs."

"Ok, I'll buzz you in—second floor."

The buzzer crackled and he pushed the door open. He started to climb the stairs two at a time when his phone rang.

"Yeah."

"Tone, it's George what's up?"

"Hey."

"Tony I saw that house on St. Lawrence you spoke about. It has a "For sale" sign on it. It looks good from the outside. Do what you can to get me in bro. I want to see that."

"Ok, what are you doing later?"

"I've gotta go meet Ray."

"Ray? For what?"

"Ah, small business. Hey, just get me into that house ok buddy? Later."

CLICK

"George?! George?! Hello?"

George had hung up. Tony thought to himself *"What business could he possibly have with Ray? Ray's not into Porsches. It's too early in the day for freaky shit."* He hit the top of the steps and knocked on the door. She opened it.

"Hi, baby", she stepped out into the corridor to greet him. She tipped-toed and swung both arms around his neck. She was overjoyed and happy to see him.

"Hey, babe."

They locked lips for a few minutes then entered the house. Tony stared at her, "Damn she so fucking beautiful", he thought to himself.

She was wearing nothing but a one-piece t-shirt and shorts combination with 5 buttons down the front for easy access in and out of it. He immediately noticed her protruding nipples.

He wondered if it was him causing the protrusion or the ambient temperature. She led him inside to the left of the corridor. The wall was adorned with frames holding pictures of her and her family posing with prominent political figures in the Clinton administration. One photo in particular grabbed his attention. It was a black and white photo of her in a sad headshot pose displaying her huge beautiful lips.

"Wow, this is a beautiful picture"

"Thank you, that was taken by a friend of mine back when I was in high school. He was in my photography class and I was his subject."

"Damn, he must've gotten an A plus on this shot."

She continued to show him the apartment. He kept looking down at her ass as it rhythmically swayed with every step she took. She led him toward the right where the entrance to the living room was. Everything was white, white sectional couches, white dining table, even a huge white bar that took up the whole right corner of the place. Tony smiled.

"Very nice" he said

"Sit down" she offered.

He sat down. She pranced in front of him and started to arrange some C.D.'s from the CD tower. He watched her and processed her every move in slow motion-the way that the one piece she was wearing grazed and pressed against her erect nipples, and the way it hugged her J-lo ass. "God what a sight." She looked at him through the corner of her eye and smiled.

"Like what you see?"

"You've got no idea. Come here let me show you how much"

"Oh yeah?" she challenged

She turned toward him, pranced over to him on the tip of her toes, and straddled him on the sofa. She put her arms around his neck and began to lick his lips and tease him. He could feel her warm fluids seep through her one piece as she grinded her pelvis onto his stiff member. He grabbed her ass cheeks and squeezed them with passion as they kissed.

He slipped both middle fingers under the moist fabric and pressed against her warm slippery chunky lips. She loved it. She let out a distinct moan of enjoyment. He flickered his fingers intensifying her pleasure. She lifted and forced herself onto his fingers causing him to finger fuck her. She opened her mouth by his ear and let out hot-aired moans into it. He started to unbutton the five buttons and pulled the top portion of the one piece off exposing her beautiful breasts. They weren't big, but they were perfect. Her nipples alone were half an inch tall and hard. He grabbed one and licked around her area before zeroing in on her stiff hard nipple. They looked and tasted like jellybeans. He started licking one nipple while sucking the other one. She squirmed and moaned, grabbed the back of his head with both hands, and pressed his head against her breast smothering him with them. He felt her kissing him on top of his head. She violently pulled his hair snapping his head back and started to kiss him again. He licked her lips outlining them with his tongue.

She slid back-giving herself enough room to unzip his pants and take out his tool. She pulled it out and started to stroke it. She slipped off his lap and knelt on the floor. She grabbed his cock with both hands and stared at him.

"Go ahead" he said.

"Do you want me to?"

"Like you wouldn't believe."

"I don't know baby my mouth is kind of dry."

Tony started laughing knowing she had him where she wanted him.

"Dry mouth makes it all the better."

"Really!" she said surprisingly.

"Yeah baby really."

She enveloped his dick with her mouth. He felt the heat from her mouth as she sucked his rock hard cock. While looking directly into his eyes she pulled back off his dick and pulled a long string of saliva from it letting it stretch then snap back right onto her bottom lip. She smiled while looking up at him.

"You like that? Not too dry?"

"From now on just make sure you have dry mouth baby."

She smiled and took him into her mouth again sucking and stroking. He was losing his mind. It felt so different and unique- way different than Kristina. His heart pounded with the same intensity that it did with Kristina, but he didn't look at Inez as he did Kristina.

Inez stepped back and the rest of the one piece she wore just dropped to her ankles. She stepped out of it and straddled him again. She grabbed his dick and held it up as she slid right into it.

"Oh Tony it feels so fucking good papi."

"Hmmm, you like that mami?"

"Ahi si papi rompeme ese toto, metemelo duro."

She hopped up and down relentlessly. Then she started grinding her pelvis onto his bone. She threw her head back and started screaming. He grabbed her ass cheeks and pulled her toward him while thrusting his cock into her, intensifying her pleasure. He stood up with her still straddled onto him and turned around. He placed her on the sofa while still inside of her. He pressed his knees against the sofa and watched as she pressed her legs open into a split. He grabbed her by the waist and pulled her into him while simultaneously thrusting into her. He watched her as she grabbed her perfect tits and squeezed them together.

"Pull off your pants papi."

He took off his pants, grabbed her again and started thrusting hard, emitting a slapping sound that came from his thighs slamming into her sweaty ass cheeks. He leaned forward and grabbed her shoulders enabling him to pull her toward him and intensifying the feeling by being able to thrust deeper.

"Ahi papi, right there, right there, right there, ahi papi, si cono, oooh, ooooooh, now! Baby now!"

She busted into a convulsing shake that startled him.

"Are you ok?" he asked

"Shhhhhhh"

She kept gyrating as she climaxed all over his hard cock. When she was done she rolled over onto the couch and lay there staring at him. He looked over at her.

"You've got something." he said

"What?"

"You've got something that I love."

"Oh yeah?" she said as she smiled"

"Well you're amazing" she said.

"Amazing?"

"Yup amazing" she replied.

They held each other for over an hour. He observed every inch of her body in that hour. She was truly a voluptuous beauty. He ran his fingers through her hair then turned her face toward his. He looked into her eyes and kissed her luscious lips very hard.

"Hmmmmmm, damn girl you've got something."

He got up, went to the bathroom, and when he opened the door to leave the bathroom she was there looking up at him. She tip-toed and hugged him.

"I'm gonna miss you" she said.

"I'm not going anywhere babe, just to my office. I've gotta go take care of some business"

"Thank you for stopping by" she said.

"No, thank you, for making it up to me."

"The pleasure was all mine, handsome"

****

Knock Knock Knock

"Who is it?"

"It's me open up"

"Hey what's up kid?"

"What's up Ray, where do you want to do this?"

"Go to the bedroom in the back, you want a drink?"

"Nah, I'm good, lets just take care of this."

"How many did you bring?"

"You wanted four right?"

"Yup, how much?"

"4 at 27 a piece that's 108"

He took out the crocodile skinned briefcase, clicked it open and started throwing stacks of money held together by rubber bands.

"Ok, here's 20, 40, 60, 80, 100, 5, 6, 7, and 8 and the steroids you wanted are here, these are on me, the syringes are in the bag."

"Ok, cool let me know when you need more."

"Alright, bro I'm outta here, hey check the windows for me, let me know if I'm clear."

He peeked after a few seconds and looked back.

"Ok, bro you're good to go."

"Alright thanks Ray."

"Okay, Georgie, later."

****

2 Months Later

"Congratulations on your new home George."

"Whew buddy, thank you for all your help Tone. We're celebrating tonight. I expect you to be there bro."

"What are we doing? Where are we going?"

"I don't know. I figure you, me, Rick, Ray, and Gina you know a little action?"

Tony didn't want to let George know that he really didn't want to party with Ray and Gina anymore. It got really old really fast. He would much rather spend his time with Kristina or Inez - in a perfect world both.

"Man, I'm gonna have to give these girls some half-assed excuse about tonight."

"By the way how are they? Which one are you bringing Tone?"

"Neither bro, you know better than that."

"Tony which one do you really want to be with? Have you even thought of that? You know, you can't keep doing this with these girls bro. They will find out bro and when they do you gonna end up without the rope or the goat-with neither. Trust me when I tell you buddy."

Tony thought about what George said and he knew that he was right. It had only been a short time and Tony already felt like he was in love with both girls. He couldn't choose.

"I know, I know I have to choose, but I don't know how to."

"Bro that's easy, eennie, meenei, miny, moe."

"Man George I wish it was that easy."

****

The party came and as usual there was Rick, Ray, Gina, George and Tony, drinking snorting and doing the usual party favors. Tony and George stuck with the usual drinks. Tony notice George and Ray interacting more than usual with extra trips to George's bedroom.

"What was the collusion?" was the question Tony wanted answered. Tony felt really uncomfortable and his not wanting to be there made it worse. In one of the trips to the room with George, Tony secretly grabbed his stuff and started to leave.

"No, no, no baby don't leave"

"Gina it's 4 am, I really gotta go."

"Pleeeaase Tony don't go."

"No sweety maybe another time, I gotta go see someone."

"Ok baby gimme a kiss" she said.

Tony kissed Gina and said bye to Rick. He got in his car and called Kristina. Her voicemail picked up. He hung up leaving no message. He called Inez immediately after and a groggy voice picked up.

"Hello?"

"Inez?"

"Yeah"

"Sorry to wake you it's me Tony."

"Hey, baby hi. I've missed you, are you ok?"

"Oh yeah hon, I just wanted to hear your voice."

"Oh baby you're so cute."

"Thank you baby, I'll call you tomorrow."

"Ok baby bye."

On his way home Tony felt better about leaving George's party. Speaking to Inez sort of took him to a satisfied place. He tried Kristina once again but voice mail came back on.

He arrived home and bathed in a hot aromatherapy induced tub. He lay there and as he did flashes of Inez and Kristina flooded his mind. Tony pondered and pondered on how he needed to decide between one of these two, but how? They were both everything he'd ever wanted in women. Whatever one lacked the other had and vice versa. One was the beautiful woman that liked the married life, sensitive, kind, beautifully thin and very reserved and discreet, then there was the other only equally as beautiful but more voluptuous, less reserved, very wild and sexually free and didn't want to get married.

He thought and thought.

"Dear god how do I choose?"

****

Knock, knock, knock

Tony got out of bed wondering who was at the door. He looked through the peephole and opened the door.

"George, what's up bro?"
"Tone my man, what's up bro?"

George entered the apartment and set a huge duffle bag on the floor. *"Bro you going on vacation?"*

"Nah, I just didn't want to leave it in the car. With my luck they'll break into my car and take my shit."

"So how was the party?"

"Oh man, you left just when the party was getting started. It was good though, those two can go for days."

"Yeah man they go at it too hard. How do you like your new house bro, are you happy?"

"Fuck yeah Tone, how about you, how's that commission check? Shit 20gs that's a nice payday ah tone?" asked George

"Yeah well that broker's test was really fucking hard bro."

Tony opened the refrigerator and was shoved out of the way by George.

"Move over bro lets see what you've got in here, daeeem Tone you sad puppy. What you got robbed for food, spend some of that commission check on food bro? I'll be back I'm going to the store to buy some stuff for this sorry ass refrigerator, be back later."

"Ok, yo bring a three liter diet Pepsi."

Forty minutes passed and George still wasn't back. Tony looked at his watch and wondered what the hell could be taking George so long. He kicked back and started watching television. Two hours

126

passed and no George.

"Where the fuck is this nigga at?", "You know who this is leave a message."
He called George on the cell but got his voice mail

"Hey George man it's been over 3 hours where you at?? Call me."

He hung up the phone and decided to leave. He opened the closet door and grabbed the duffle bag, the weight of the bag nearly ripped his arm out of the socket. He then dragged it to the closet.

"Man, what the fuck is in here?"

With all the strength he could muster he hauled the bag and tossed it into the closet.

RING RING

"Hello?"

"Tony?"

"Nigga where the fuck are you bro?"

"Hey I'm sorry bro, I just got called I have to fly out to Miami in two hours."

"What for?"

"Business bro."

"Ok, I'll drive you where you at?"

"I'm already on the van back to the airport."

"Bro how about this bag?"

"Yeah about that bag, dude you're the only one I would trust with a bag like that so hold onto that for me. I'll pick it up when I get back. Hey I left something for you in the kitchen drawer."

"When are you coming back bro?"

"Couple of days."

"Shit, ok call me when you get in" said Tony.

"Alright."

Tony hung up the phone and looked at the closet. He thought and thought.

"What the fuck is in that bag that's so heavy." He fought the urge to go check what was in the bag and just left.

****

KNOCK KNOCK KNOCK

"Who is it?"

"It's me"

"Me who?"

"Me Lilly."

The door opened and there stood Inez in a long t-shirt with no pants on. She leaned against the door.

"Hi" said Inez.

"Hi baby how are you?" Lilly, wanting to jump all over Inez, held back as per Freddy's instructions. *"Let it work, let it work you'll be irresistible to her, just let her come to you"* she remembered.

"Ok, and yourself?"

"Fine I've been thinking about you."

"Oh yeah, what about, Lilly?"

"Oh, you know what we had."

Lilly noticed Inez's head tilt slightly, a sign that Inez was warming up to Lilly's advances.

"Oh shit can this be working already?" Lilly thought to herself. Inez smiled.

"Yeah what we had was nice, but Lily you're out of control."

Lilly stared at her ready to give in, *"Fuck fuck fuck I'm breaking protocol"* she thought to herself.

"Anyway listen baby I came by to ask you, are you still in touch with that guy Tony?"

"Yes very much so, why?"

"Because I never got the chance to thank him for making sure I was all right that night that he took me to the hospital."

"I'd like to thank him by taking you both out for dinner and drinks. Nothing formal just a casual thing, how about it?"

"Really?" Inez asked suspiciously.

"That's not like you to do something like that."

"Ohhhh , damn Inez that's fucked up."

"I'm serious, that's not like you, either way that's a nice gesture, thank you. I'll call him and ask him to see how he feels about it."

129

"Tell him at Mystiques-the place where we all met."

"Ok, I'll tell him."

Inez looked at Lilly with suspicion but also with goo goo eyes, Lilly, barely containing herself, walked away.

"Ok, baby let me know ok?" asked Lilly.

"Alright honey."

Lilly exited the house sporting a huge grin. She knew her plan was coming together nicely.

****

Lilly's cell phone rang.

"Hello?"

"Hey it's me Inez."

"Hey baby what's up?

"I called Tony and he agreed to go out for some drinks but he doesn't want to go to Mystiques."

"Wow that was fast, ok, so we'll go to a small place I know called 718 Lounge over on Tremont ave."

"Ok, he said Friday was good."

"Ok then Friday it is."

"Ok, bye baby."

****

Three days had passed and there hadn't been a moment that Tony hadn't thought about opening that bag. He was sitting there with a glass of Godiva white liquor, staring at the plasma TV that hung on his wall. Playing on the screen was "The Thomas Crown Affair".

Tony's eyes shifted from the plasma, to the closet, to the plasma repeatedly. He slowly sat up while staring at the closet. He took a deep breath as if he were about engage in a gun battle. He muted the sound that poured out of the Bose surround sound system. Other than the heavy alcohol induced breaths that blew out of his nostrils everything was silent.

He placed his glass on the center table creating a clinging sound that occurred when two pieces of glass come together.

He took another deep breath and stood up off the blue velour couch. Underestimating the effects of the liquor, his head spun like a tornado. He stuck out his arms to find his balance while his eyes locked on the closet. He took a step toward the closet then another until he reached the door. He pulled the handle and the door swung open revealing the duffle bag. Dizzy and off balance Tony addressed the bag.

"We meet again, what are you hiding inside of you?" Tony yelled in his worse Scarface accent ever.

He pulled the bag through one of it's handles and it slid out of the closet in a drunken rage he grabbed the zipper....................

"BZZZZ BZZZZZ BZZZZZ" buzzer buzzed. Tony stammered to the intercom.

"Who is it?!"

"It's me George buzz me up!"

"Who?"

131

"George bro!"

Tony pressed the button and let George up. He knocked and Tony opened.

"Whoa! Tone you ok bro? Look at you bro you are drunk"

Tony stammered and slurred "Ahhh, I'm not drunk, where the hell did you go? And what the hell is in that bag?!" Tony yelled

"Whooa whoa Tone easy with the yelling buddy some things are better left unknown, but if it makes you feel any better I left an envelope in your kitchen drawer, don't you remember? I told you when you called me three days ago wondering where I went."

George walked over to the drawer and pulled out the envelope. He handed it to Tony.

"What the hell is this?" Tony slurred.

He opened the envelope and pulled out ten crisp one-hundred dollar bills. Tony looked up at George.

"What's this for?"

"Well to be honest with you Tone, I knew I was going out of town this morning. I just didn't know at what time. So I figured when they called me I'd just take off, but I wasn't expecting to be in the elevator on the way up here, and since I was already in your house I figured I'd just use the empty refrigerator as an excuse to leave and leave the bag here-but not before leaving the envelope in the drawer. It's a sort of a thank you for holding a half million dollars for me"

"Half a million dollars? !Half a million dollars?! Half a million fucking dollars?" Tony ran to the bag and unzipped it himself to see it with his own eyes. There stood endless stacks of 20's, 50's and 100's Tony looked up at George.

"Bro, I wont even ask" said Tony.

"You upset bro?"

"Well you're fucked up for not telling me what's up and leaving me with this bag loaded with a half mil. I could've stashed it somewhere safer."

"You're right, sorry bro."

"Is it your money?"

"Yes, It's part of the money I was going to use for our club."

"Where did you get it? And if it is yours why don't you have it in an account somewhere or in a safer place than a duffle bag?"

"Oh shit bro, I gotta go pick up my son, I'll call you tomorrow we'll talk about it then. Keep the money in the envelope bro, later."

****

Friday night 7:30pm

RING RING

"Hello?"

"Inez?"

"Hey, baby what's up, are you ready?"

"Yeah hun, I'm downstairs waiting."

She ran to the terrace and peeked out. She saw the white beast and waved.

"Ok I'll be right down."

Tony sat in the white beast thinking about the half a million dollars that he was staring at the night before. He knew George was up to something but he couldn't put his finger on it. Flashes of all those bills went in and out of his mind.

CLICK. The door opened. "Hey you". She slid in and planted those huge lips on Tony.

"Hey beautiful, look at you, you look gorgeous."

"Thank you baby, I love that jacket" said Inez.

Tony was wearing a motorcycle jacket - aged leather the kind that fit like a glove. They took off and headed toward the lounge to meet with Lilly. They arrived and parked. Tony got out of his car and rounded the white beast to open the door for Inez. He took her hand and helped her out of the car.

"Thank you" she said.

He shut the door and they entered hand in hand. The bar was a huge semi-circle on the left. To the right couches and small round tables that light up. In the back toward the left there was a white room with a huge couch and sheer curtains. Inez led Tony toward the back where they were seated by a waitress. They ordered drinks while they waited on Lilly to arrive.

"So why the change of heart by your ex?"

"I don't know baby but she seemed sincere."

"Really? Out of left field just like that?"

"Well that's what she came at me with babe."

"Hmmm what does she really want? Seems to me like she just wants to see you."

Torn

"Then why invite you and offer to buy you drinks and all that?"

"I don't know babe I just don't .... OUCH!" Inez kicked Tony under the table.

"You just don't know what?" asked Lilly from behind Tony.

Tony got up and turned around.

"Oh hey Lilly how are you? Thank you for the invite."

Tony gave Lilly a little cheek kiss and cleaned the footprint that Inez left on his pant leg.

"So you don't know what Tony?" Lilly persisted.

"Huh? What?"

"When I walked in behind you I heard you say 'I just don't know babe' so my question is you just don't know what?"

"Oh I was telling Inez that I don't know what to do, regarding a client of mine, that's all."

Lilly looked at Inez and she nodded in confirmation then smiled.

"Tony I asked Inez to bring you here so that we can all enjoy each other and so that I can thank you for possibly saving my life."

Tony stared at her with suspicion.

"Yeah Lilly no problem. I'm positively sure you would've done the same thing for me had the situation been reversed."

Lilly picked up her glass and gestured a toast. They all lifted their glasses and Lilly spoke.

"To friendship and threesomes."

Tony looked at Inez and whispered under the music,

"Threesomes?"

Inez opened her eyes and shrugged her shoulders. She didn't know where it was coming from. The waitress came by and brought over another bottle of Moet. Tony stood up and took off his jacket, placed it behind the chair and poured the girls another round. They drank and joked for the next two hours. Tony also noticed how hard Lilly was trying now to show her feelings, but she was no match for Tony. He read right through her. Tony was sharp and perceptive. In the past half hour he caught Lilly making goo goo eyes at Inez six times.

"Excuse me ladies I need to use the rest room."

He got up grabbed his cell phone and headed toward the men's room. Once inside he hit a u-turn and cracked the door open. He had a clean view of them both. His suspicions were right. She just wanted to be around Inez. He watched as Lilly place her hand over Inez's and caressed it. He flipped open his phone and dialed Inez. Her phone vibrated, she looked at it and saw "TONY" flashing on the lcd screen.

"Hello?"

"Inez I'm in the bathroom. Listen to me very carefully get up and go to the women's bathroom. Leave her at the table. Tell her you have to take this personal call."

"Okay."

She got up and told Lilly that she would be back. She entered the women's bathroom.

"Baby, what's up?"

Tony closed the door and went back inside.

"Yo, I think this bitch wants me here just so I can watch her make passes at you."

"Baby nooo."

"Are you kidding me? Are you telling me that you didn't see what I saw?"

"Oh no I caught it, I was just hoping you didn't."

"Well you didn't think I was that stupid did you?"

"No baby I just wanted to give her the benefit of the doubt, I really thought the gesture was genuine."

"Alright babe another half hour and that's it."
"Ok, honey."

"See you at the table."

Inez headed to the table and saw Lilly hanging up the phone.

"Another girlfriend?" asked Inez.

"Yeah."

Tony turned to use the urinal, he started relieving himself when he heard the commotion outside. He hurried and zipped up. He grabbed the door handle, pulled it open, and was startled to find three men standing there. They all turned toward him.

"FREEZE! Motherfucker!"

Tony threw his hands in the air.

"Get up against the bar, spread your legs!"

They were all against the bar. The music came to a screeching halt.

The men had badges hanging off their chest.

"This is a raid. Don't do anything stupid and everything's gonna be alright."

Two of the men went behind the bar and started turning the back of the bar and the register upside down. Tony looked to his left and saw two burley cops blocking the door. He looked to his right and saw three other guys frisking bags and jackets at the tables. Tony looked down at the floor and damned himself for accepting that invitation from Lilly.

"Who's fucking jacket is this?"

No answer, Tony was still looking down at the floor.

"I said who does this jacket belong to?"

Tony looked up and turned his face toward where the voice came from. What he saw then turned him white and numb. The officer stood there displaying the leather jacket in his right hand and in the left hand a large zip lock bag filled 3/4 way with white powder, the officer saw Tony's demeanor.

"Yo you, is this yours?"

"The jacket is mine but that other shit is not."

"So how did it get in your pocket, cuff him lets go."

Tony in a panic threw his phone at Inez who was as shocked as he was.

"Baby call George and tell him what happened. Tell him to send a lawyer."

"Shut up, turn around and spread em asshole!"

Torn

****

1/2 Hour later Inez scrolled down the electronic phonebook on Tony's cell phone looking for George's number. While scrolling down, the phone started to violently vibrate and startled Inez.
Kristina's name started to flash on the LCD screen. Inez's head started to race. Who is she? Sister, cousin, another girl, friend from work? She blocked the thoughts and continued to scroll for George. She found it and called.

"This is George leave a message."

"Hi, George my name is Inez. Listen I'm sorry to call you so late, but I was with Tony tonight and he was arrested. He asked me to call you for a lawyer, I have his phone please call me back on it, thanks."

She hung up and grabbed a piece of paper. She started jotting down Kristina's number.

****

Friday night Clevelander Hotel Miami Beach

George's phone just stopped ringing.

"Baby who was that?"

"Tony."

"Why didn't you answer the phone?"

"Babe, did you want me to stop eating you out just to pick up the fuckin phone?"

"Ooooh, I would've tossed your phone in the toilet"

"Well there you go. That's why I didn't pick up the phone"

"Well are you gonna call him back?

"Jesus girl, you're worried more about Tony's call than I am. What is it does he fuck you better?"

Dead silence filled the room. You could cut the tension with a knife. The phone rang again. George ignored it and headed into the shower. She tip toed to the phone and saw Tony's name flashing on and off.

"Babe, It's Tony," she shouted.

"What the fuck, pick it up then and invite him over for a threesome if you want, Fuck!"

She grabbed the phone and brought it to the bathroom,

"Here pick it up. It could be important."

"Tone what's up brother?"

"Hi George please?"

"Why do you have Tony's phone?"

"My name is Inez and I'm calling because I was with Tony tonight. He was arrested and asked me to called you for a lawyer."

"What? Did you say they arrested him? For what?"

"I think it was for drugs."

"Drugs, that cant be, Tone doesn't do any of that shit."

"Well they raided the place we were at and when they checked his jacket he had coke on him."

"Tone doesn't do or sell drugs, are you sure?"

Torn

"Yes, I was there!"

"Where did they take him?"

"I think 161st."

"Ok thank you I'll take care of it"

"Can you please call me and let me know what happens."

"Ok, Bye."

****

"Listen honey, these guys nowadays are just bums baby. You were in love with a drug-dealing loser and you're just lucky they didn't stop you guys in a traffic stop. If not you'd be right there with him" said Lilly.

"Lilly please just take me home. It doesn't make sense. I need time to find out what happened and make sense of all this."

"Ok, honey."

Lilly drove Inez home. As Inez started making her way out of the car, she paused for a second, put both hands up to her face and broke down in tears. Lilly put her arms around her, held her and softly caressed her.

"sh sh sh, it's ok honey, it'll be fine."

She wiped her tears and stepped out of the car.

"Sorry Lilly I've gotta go."

"Ok baby, good night."

The door slammed shut and Lilly took off. She picked up her cell phone and called her padrino.

"Hello?"

"Hi Freddy, it's me Lilly."

"Aiee nena did they show up?"

"Yeah padrino they found the stuff, I put it in the jacket and they arrested him."

He let out a wicked laugh.

"Listen nena the first thing you have to do is attack her, now that she's vulnerable. He'll probably make bail on Monday so you have to take advantage of this weekend. On Monday you have to come and give thanks to your santos for being with you, which reminds me, I have to thank my nephew for arresting our little thorn. I'll see you Monday, ok nena?"

"Ok padrino, thank you for everything, bye."

She made a sharp u-turn and returned to Inez's house. She parked and waited until the one light that was lit in the bedroom was turned off. When it did she made her move. She went in and knocked on the door. Inez opened.

"Hi, I came back because I thought you could use the company. Besides, you shouldn't have to be alone at a time like this" said Lilly.

"Lilly, I told you I'll be fine."

Lilly reached out, put her hand on Inez's shoulder and gently massaged her.

"C'mon baby you know I love you, and you know no man can make you feel the way I can baby."

Torn

Inez fell under Lilly's seductive moves and invited her in.

****

Clevelander Hotel, Miami Beach

"Shit, I gotta get him outta there man!"

He grabbed his cell phone and dialed Ray's number.

"Hello?"

"Ray?"

"George what's up bro?"

"Yo Ray I'm caught up bro, I need you to do me a favor."

"Talk to me bro what do you need?"

"Tony got locked up tonight and we need to bail him out. I would but I'm in P.R. I need for you to handle those lawyer fees if you can and when I get back I'll take care of you."

"No problem I got it. I'm waiting for my wife to call. She's at her moms out in Philly then I go."

"Okay bro thanks. Listen the lawyer can't do nothing till Monday so just make sure that Monday morning you're there first thing."

"Alright bro."

George hung up the phone, put his head down, and looked over to watch as she combed her hair in the mirror.

"What did he say?" she asked

"He said he'd take care of it. He's waiting for your call, so call him

143

now."

"Why now?"

"Because you told him you'd call him from your mom's house and you didn't. The longer you take to call him back, the longer Tony sits in a jail cell."

She grabbed her phone and started to dial.

"Hey honey?"

"Hey baby what's up what are you doing?"

"Oh nothing, on my way to my brothers house with my mom."

"Alright look I gotta hang up. I need to call a lawyer for Tony, he got locked up last night."

Gina, putting on her best Oscar performance, acted surprised.

"Oh my God, why? What happened?"

"I'll explain everything to you when you get home."

"Ok, honey I love you."

"Love you too, bye."

****

Saturday Morning

Ray bolted out the door to meet the attorney. His phone rang. He looked at the caller ID and it displayed a 305 number. Curious and surprised he picked up the phone.

"Hello?"

Torn

"Ray, it's me Brandon."

"Oh shit Brandon, man, I'm sorry bro. I was meaning to call you months ago to cancel what we had going. Since I hired you we've renewed our vows and my relationship with my wife has been stronger than ever. Things are going well. Don't worry though I'll pay you everything I owe you since we started, how much is the total?"

"Well Ray my friend I'm afraid I can't do that, my investigation is not over."

"What do you mean it's not over? I'm ending it right now, it's over."

"You may not want to do that just yet my friend. Do you know where I'm at right now?"

"It's a 305 area-that's Miami"

"That's right South Beach buddy, only I'm not on vacation."

"We'll I'm sorry to hear that Brandon, but that has nothing to do with me."

"Well then, can you explain to me why I'm looking at your wife right now in a terra cotta colored 2 piece bikini with another man whom I've never seen before?"

"What?!" Ray yelled.

"That's right Ray, when you asked me to cancel, I never stopped following her. My suspicions were the same as yours. It was only a matter of time, but she's not my wife. That's why I didn't want to agree with you when you thought she was clean, so I kept following her. She's been shacked up at the Clevelander Hotel for the past 2 days and she just left with this dude 10 minutes ago."

"What does he look like?"

"I couldn't get a good look at him he wore a like a fisherman's kind of hat with shades. He knows how to hide so I couldn't get a clear shot of him, but I did get some photos maybe you can recognize him from one of them."

"That scumbag bitch! She told me she was at her mothers house!"

"I hate to be the bearer of bad news but that's what you pay me for."

"Brandon, just send me these pictures as soon as possible."

"Will do, bro."

Ray dialed the attorney.

"Hello, attorney's office?"

"Hi, Tommy Lee Please?"

"Hold on please."

"This is Tommy."

"Tommy, hey listen I'm on my way to see you regarding a friend of mine who got locked up and needs representation."

"What's his name?"

"Antonio Falcon."

"Ok, I'll find him, bring $5000 and we'll go from there."

"Ok, I'll be there in 10 minutes, bye."

"Bye."

****

Monday morning

Tony exited the building known as 500 Pearl St. NY, NY. The horn blared twice. Tony turned to see Ray waiting out there for him. Tony wearing an old T-shirt, khaki institution pants, and a pair of blue skippies rushed to the car.

"Man Ray am I glad to see you. Thank you bro."

"No problem bro, thank George. He was the one who called me and ask me to bail you out."

"Where is he?"

"He's in P.R."

"How's Gina?"

"Man tone I just found out, that bitch is fucking around behind my back."

"What?!" Tony asked

"Yeah man, I don't know with who though."

"Well let's hire a P.I."

"I did man, I hired one a year ago and I forgot he was still on the case. Shit I haven't paid the guy in about 8 months, then he called me, I thought it was to collect......"

"Then he broke it to you" Tony said.

"Yeah bro, he'll have some photos for me but it won't be for a couple of weeks."

"Well what are we going to do with this guy when we find him?"

" I don't know Tone."

"Well just let me know what we have to do and well do it."

"Thanks."

****

Tony got home and jumped in the shower, something he lacked for the past three days. After a three-hour bath soak he called her.

"Hello?"

"Hey Inez?"

"Yeah, how are you?"

"I'm glad to be home, to hear your voice."

"Hmmmm", she said with an attitude"

"What's up I sense some attitude."

"So Tony, since when have you been dealing drugs?"

"Inez you can't be fucking serious."

"Oh no, and why not?"

"Inez I don't sell or do drugs"

"So explain to me what happened Friday night?"

"Somebody put that shit in my pocket, Inez"

"Oh Tony please what do you think this is a movie?"

"Inez, please I know it must have been that bitch Lilly. It had to be. I didn't have that on me when I left my house and all of a sudden it

was there. C'mon baby don't be so naïve, remember when we were in the bathroom?"

"Why? She has no motive, no reason. Why?"

"Oh no please tell me you didn't. Please tell me you didn't hook up with that witch after that happened? Tell me you didn't give in?"

There was silence.

"Inez, please don't tell me."

It hit Inez like a ton of bricks.

"She seduced you, didn't she? Wait don't tell me, she spent the night too right? Feel free to stop me when I'm wrong."

"What the fuck Tony, how was I supposed to know?"

"It's easy Inez, find out the facts before you accuse anyone of anything and don't do anything stupid."

Inez knew right away that Tony was telling the truth. She stood on the line in silence.

"Do you still have my cell phone?"

"Yes."

"When I get a chance I'll pick it up"

He hung up the phone without giving her a chance to respond. He picked up the phone and dialed Kristina.

"Hello?"

"Kristina?"

"Yeah."

"Hi it's me Tony."

"Hi sweety, I'm so sorry I haven't called you. I've been swamped at work. I've been working 12 to 15 hour days and when I'm not working I'm sleeping. So what's up baby?"

"I miss you honey."

"Oh yeah?"

"Yeah, when am I going to see your face?" asked Kristina.

"Come stay with me tonight. I need you here, I just got home from jail."

"What, jail. For what?"

"It's a long story baby, I'll tell you when you get here."

"Okay, bye."

****

Midnight that night

The door and phone went off at the same time.

"Who is it?"

"Me Kristina."

He opened the door and let her in, while he answered the phone.

"Hello?"

"Tone, George what's up, are you ok?"

150

Torn

"Shit bro, thanks for hooking up with Ray to get me out."

"Don't mention it bro. What the hell happened?"

"They raided this place and found coke in my pocket."

"Nigga, since when do you do coke?" George asked surprisingly.
"No bro my jacket was on the chair, and when they raided the place they found the stuff in the jacket. When they asked 'who does the jacket belong to' I owned up to it not knowing what it had in it. I was set up bro."

"Bro but who would want to set you up?"

"Well look bud, Kristina is here so we'll hook up tomorrow ok?"

"Oh, ok I got it, aight Tone"

Kristina looked over at Tony.

"Honey why would anyone want to set you up, and who were you with that they didn't look out for you?"

"Babe I was out with some Investors who were making a proposition for a club partnership and they were also interested in buying some commercial property."

"Oh my poor baby."

She caressed his face and started giving him small pecks of love on his forehead, cheeks, and lips. They slowly undressed each other and made passionate love all night.

****

Inez was sitting on her bed when she heard keys jingling at the door. The door opened and closed. Lilly walked down the corridor and took a left into the kitchen. She started to prepare dinner. Inez crept

151

out of her room. Her face had tears and black mascara running down her cheeks. She held her fists tightly as she approached the kitchen. She turned left and put her hands behind her back. She stood there in silence just staring at Lilly as she cut cubes of steak. Inez stared at Lilly's back as it moved gracefully. She turned around, saw Inez, dropped her knife and took Inez into her arms.

"Oh my God baby what happened are you alright? Why are you crying, is everything ok?"

In one swift motion Inez swung her arm from behind and plunged a 12-inch chef's knife into Lilly's abdomen. Lilly grabbed Inez's forearm as she fell to her knees. She looked up at Inez's eyes.

"Why? Inez I love you."

Freddy jumped from his bed in a panic.

"Aye dios mio, my god, aye perdoname. Aye Lilly where are you cono, aye, aye, aye"

He ran to the phone and dialed Lilly's cell phone number.

"Hello?"

"Lilly?"

"Yeah?"

"Aye dios mio gracias a dios, Thank god, nena are you? ...."

"Padrino calm down, Whats the matter?"

"Aye nena I just had the worst dream, that Inez killed you."

"What..?"

"Si, yes you have to come and see me right now, tengo que

despojarte. I have to give you something nena, because things don't look good for you and her."

"Padrino what are you talking about? We're just fine."

"When was the last time you spoke to her?"

"Last week when I spent the night."

"Then what?"

"Then nothing. She's good trust me. I think that Tony guy is still in jail. I stuck enough of that stuff in his pocket to keep him there a while."

"No, no, no nena you were supposed to keep working her everyday, don't give the spell a chance to wear off. Cono, you're just like a man. You sleep with her then don't call her for a week. Anything could've happened in a week."

"So what do I do?"

"Come see me today after work."

"Ok."

Lilly disconnected the call and immediately called Inez.

"Hello?" Inez answered

"Baby, hi"

"Listen you bitch, how could you have done what you did and expect me not to find out?!"

"What are you talking about Inez?"

"You know what I'm talking about you conniving little bitch. You

*spend the night with me and made all these promises to me about
how you love me and want to be with me forever, how this guy Tony
and all these guys were bums and losers when it was your lying
sneaky ass who set him up. How could you do that to someone who
saved your life? You selfish bitch, you ruined his life!"*

*"Whoa, Inez slow down, I may have been guilty of not calling for a
week, but believe me baby I had nothing to do with setting him up."*

"Yeah ok, look just forget about me alright?!"

"Inez, wait, I didn't set him up, he's a drug dealing coke head!"

"How the fuck are you so fucking sure? You don't even know him!"

"Trust me I know!"

"Trust you, ha, you don't know shit!"

Inez cut the call and left Lilly dangling on her words. Lilly knew it
was over. She was done.

****

Tony arrived at his office where he was greeted by his secretary.

*"Hi Tony, here are your messages, 27 from Inez, 9 are from buyers,
and 7 from sellers. Oh and this young lady dropped off your phone. I
think it was the 27 message girl."*

"Yeah, must have been. Thank you Maria."

He grabbed his messages and phone, entered his office and started
returning calls. His last call was to Ray.

"Hey Ray what's going on?"

"Nothing Tone."

Torn

"How's it been going? You know with the wife and all?"

"Well I'm trying to keep it low key she doesn't know that I know and I don't want to say anything until I see the pictures. I've been fighting my urges to stick my foot so far up her ass I'll see my toes through her mouth."

"When do you get the pictures?"

"Today at 7 p.m."

"Whoa, I'm there bro wait for me."

"Yeah bring George so you guys can help me figure this shit out."

"Alright bro, I'll see you later."

****

Inez in a last ditch effort to get Tony to respond, pulled out the piece of paper that she had with Kristina's number on it and dialed.

"Hello you have reached Kristina…"

Inez hung up.

That evening Tony and George arrive at Ray's house. They knocked and Ray let them in.

"Fellas fellas, what's up, come in."

"Ray how are you feeling man?" asked Tony.

"He's good Tone, he's stronger than he thinks" interrupted George.

"Man, I'm hoping those picture are of some other woman and this guy is wrong" said Ray.

155

"Do you have any clue of who this guy might be?" asked George

"No man no clue, I didn't even know anything until this P.I. called me letting me know that he was still on the case. I would've never known anything."

The intercom buzzed.

"That must be him!" Ray was excited but nervous.

"Oh, shit, I've gotta get outta here" said George.

"What? Whoa whoa whoa wait up! Ray needs us right now bro, don't be a dick" Tony said.

Ray opened the door and let Brandon in. Brandon held a large yellow manila envelope in his hand. George's eyes stayed glued on that envelope like it was a bomb.

"So Mr. Brandon what do I owe you?"

"The bill is $6,000."

"Will you take a check?"

"Yes."

"Look Brandon I want to thank you for your time and energy since you kept going when I told you to stop."

"Look man I'm sorry I always feel horrible when I have to deliver this type of crushing information. I'm really sorry."

"Thank you."

"I'll leave you now. Thanks guys."

"Later" said George.

Torn

"Later" said Tony.

Ray shut the door and turned to look at the guys.

"Well this is it fellas."

They all hudled over the kitchen Island and started opening the envelope. He pulled the pictures out and sure enough there she was in a 2 piece terra cotta bathing suit, walking on Ocean Drive hand in hand with a guy wearing a hat, shades, cargo shorts and flip flops. His head was tilted down. He was unrecognizable to Ray or Tony it was almost as if he knew he was being photographed. George knew it was him.

A tear ran down ray's cheek.

"Look fellas I really gotta go, I'm sorry about everything Ray, call me so we can take care of that."

Ray Looked at George and nodded, George left. He ran downstairs and jumped into the yellow beast. He grabbed his phone and dialed Gina.

"Hello you've reached G I'm not in at the moment please leave a message"

"Gina your husband knows you're having an affair, I just left your house, he doesn't know it's me but he has pictures of you call me back."

He takes off and rushes down to the city, bobbing and weaving in and out of traffic in an effort to catch her at work. 30 minutes later he pulled up to the penthouse gentleman's club located at west end and 21st. He saw 4 beautiful young ladies out front.

"Good evening ladies, I'm looking for Gina, I think she works here do any of you know her?"

"Yeah" says one of the bombshells

"She left about 30 minutes ago"

"Yeah she was pissed, her purse was stolen with her money and her phone" said the buxom brunette.

George put his head down, he tried but it was too little too late.

****

"Can you tell who it is?"

"no man, but the style of dress is very familiar." said Tony *"I trusted that bitch, that fucking whore.!*

"hey, hey Ray relax bro, I know this is not…"

The conversation was interrupted by the keys jingling at the door locks. Ray leapt toward the door, grabbed the door knob and forcefully opened the door, as he did she was pulled in as she held onto the key which was still in the lock. He grabbed her hair with his right hand and with his left hand he plunged his fist into her mouth, causing blood to splatter all over the walls.

"No no no no Ray!" Tony shouted Tony jumped onto Gina shielding her from any more of the damaging blows that Ray was throwing her way.

"You fucking whore, you piece of shit, how could you do this to me?!"

He grabbed the envelope and tossed it toward her hitting her in the face. The photos rained all over the floor. She placed her hand over her mouth trying to contain the blood.

She put her head down and started crying. Ray rushed out and slammed the door.

158

Torn

****

Tony knelt down, picked Gina up into his arms and carried her into the bedroom. He laid Her down, she cried endlessly. He went into the bathroom and drew warm water in the tub for her. He returned to the room, undressed her and carried her naked into the bathroom and gently placed her into the bathtub.

" Why can't he be like you Tony?"

"I don't know Gina People are different"

"All he ever wants to do is sniff, fuck and take all those fucking drugs!"

"sh sh sh sh sh c'mon Gina relax stop crying"

"No no Tony, do you know that he can't even get it up unless he sees you fucking me?"

"Stop Gina don't say that."

Tony tilted her torso forward and began to wash her back.

"Tony it's true the motherfucker is a dead dick, he can't fuck unless someone is fucking me"

""Gina stop" Tony knodded

"I wish he was like you, Tony."

"Please Gina, my life is a shit storm, I'm probably more fucked up than he is. I've got my own mess."

He tilted her back and handed her the soap.

"Here babe you do the front."

"Do it for me honey"

"No Gina, then I'm Gonna get crazy and we don't want nothing to happen here" said Tony

"Why, it's not like you've never fucked me before, Shit I think you've fucked me more than my own husband."

"Gina I promised your husband I would never do anything unless he were here with us"

"Please Tony, he won't find out"

"No, Gina!"

"Damn Tony George wasn't like that"

Tony stood still, then It hit him, the cargo pants, Flip flops that style. He jumped off his knees and ran out of the bathroom, picked the pictures up from the floor and stared at them, Now he saw it.

"George!"

****

George met Ray to take care of business.

"Hey man you ok?"

"AAggrrh! Fuck!, that bitch, George I don't know what I'm gonna do!"

"Hey look Ray if you want to postpone this deal, lets put it off."

"Na man we're already here, do you have the shit?"

"Yeah, I got it." They go both to the front of the yellow, George opens the hood and pulls out the bag.

"there you go bro 20 bricks."

Ray grabbed the bag and handed George another bag that he pulled from his trunk.

"Here George there's 370 I'm 30 grand short. I'll be in Miami next week to pick up your 30 grand. Don't worry I'll fly you out and we can make a little vacation out of it."

"You got it buddy"

"I'll call you during the week bro" said ray

"Ok.....Hey Ray keep your chip up buddy."

They got into their cars and headed In opposite directions.

****

Sunday Morning

Tony is awakened by the ringing phone.

"Hello?" he asks in a half dead tone

"Good morning my beautiful stranger"

"Hey, what's up, how about a little breakfast and pampering?" Kristina asked

"Yeah ok, what do you have in mind?"

" Pick me up in an hour" she asked

"ok. Bye"

Tony got up and prepared himself. Within the hour Kristina was in the passengers seat of the white beast.

"Honey, you want to eat or pamper first?"

"Are you hungry,?" he asked

"Not really" she replied
"Ok we'll pamper first god knows I need it." He said

"Oh baby what's the matter?"

"Oh man, I'm stressed over some shit that George did."

"What happened?"

"George is fucking rays wife and I feel bad because I introduced them."

"Oh, look baby right there a parking spot" she interrupted.

He pulled into the spot and started to park when Kristina's phone rang.

"hello?"

"hello who's this?" the voice said

"Who am I, who are you? You're calling my phone"

"Yo, I think it's fucked up that your man Tony is Fuckin around with my girl

And playing the both of you."

"Tony, who, my Tony?"

Tony looked at her with concern. His body felt cold, he knew something was wrong. The call went dead. Kristina looked over at

Torn

Tony.

"who the hell was that?"

"Tony?" Kristina asked

"What Kristi?"

"Tony please"

"Kristina what?"

"Tony I'm only gonna ask you this question one time"

"What Kristina?"

"Tony are you seeing someone else besides me?"

"No, Kristina, why would you ask me something like that and who the fuck was that on the phone?"

"That was some bitch on the phone saying that it's fucked up how Tony was stringing along 2 girls and they both think the world of this piece of shit."

"What?"

"Yeah Tony so I'll ask you again ..."

"No need to Kristina the answer is no!"

He pulled out of the parking spot and started to drive Kristina home. Tony knew his days of having his cake and eating it too were numbered. He dropped her off and headed home.

****

Kristina pacing around her living room grabbed her cell phone and redialed the number.

"Hello?"

"Hello who's this?"

"This is Inez."

"Inez did you call my phone earlier?"

"Who's this?"

"This is Kristina."

"No, that was a friend of mine, but now that I have you on the line what's your relation to Tony?" asked Inez

"Tony is my man." Kristina said *"Really?, are you sure we're talking about the same Tony?"* asked Inez

"I don't know, what does he look like?"

"He's a stripper, he has black hair, he does a Zorro routine…"

"Real Estate broker, has a white Porsche and he's a personal trainer?" Kristina chimed in.

"Yup that's him, that asshole" said Inez

"Inez, if you don't mind my asking, how long have you been with Tony because according to him I was "The One".

"The One? Really well we've been dating over a year"

"Over a year? That son of a bitch, listen Inez do you think we can meet, I'd really like to put an end to all this mother fuckers lies."

"Yeah we can do that, when were you thinking?"

Torn

"Tomorrow, the sooner the better" Kristina said *"Fine"*

****

Knock Knock, Tony opened the door, George was standing there.

"Come in bro"
"Why the long face?" asked George

Tony turned and walked away.

"Yo yo tone, what's up bro"

Tony turned and pointed his finger at Georges face.

"You fucking asshole why did you have to cross the line,? You fucking jerk off."

"Whoa bro, back off what's up with that, what's up your ass?"

"I'm talking about Gina, you fucking sneak! You could've fucked her all you wanted as long as he was there, but no, you wanted to fuck her alone right, huh? So tell me what was the big fucking difference fucking her when he wasn't there?"

George stared at the floor, he had no answer he knew Tony was right. He sat down, crossed his fingers and put his head down.

"Damn it George, you know he doesn't have a clue it's you and you're fuckin lucky. If he ever found out you'd be in a trunk of a Cadillac with your dick cut off. Why is it that men are never ever satisfied, never happy, they always want more and more, Fuck!"

George just stood there and looked up at Tony.

"Sounds real strong what you're feeling, bro you sure it's just me that's bothering you?"

165

"What are you talking about?" Tony asked

"I know you buddy spill it."

"Inez and Kristina spoke today bro"

"Nooo man, for real? I knew it, no goat and no rope, fuck. What are you going to do?"

"I don't know George I can't do anything unless I know what's going on."

"Man " Aight bro, later."

I feel for you bro, if you need anything just call me. It's late man, I gotta go."

Tony let George out, locked up and got ready for bed.

****

Monday 11am

Kristina called Inez.

"Hello?"

"Hi Inez, this is Kristina where can I meet you?"

"I'm home you can come here"

"O.k. no problem."

Inez gave Kristina her address. Kristina called her mother to keep her company.

Knock knock.

They knocked on the door and Inez opened. They were anticipating this moment since the first day they spoke on the phone. Inez took one look at Kristina and thought to herself "you skinny anorexic bitch." Not that Kristina was anorexic, she was just skinnier than Inez. Kristina took one good look at Inez and immediately thought to herself "this fat bitch." Not that Inez was fat, it was just that Inez had the voluptuousness that Kristina didn't. They continued their catty thoughts until Inez broke the silence.

"Hi, come in."

Kristina and her mother both entered the house and took a left down the corridor, then a right into the living room.

"This is my mother my sister and my friend Lilly."

"Hello, this is my mother." Kristina said

They all shook hands as they introduced themselves. They sat down and an awkward silence came over them.

"Ok, enough of this, Lets get this over with, you girls want apple martinis?" interrupted Inez' mom

They all said yes and then it began.

"So tell me, what is it that he does with you?" asked Kristina

"He takes me on long drives, we go to the movies, picnics we do a lot of little things here at home. He does a lot of small thoughtful beautiful things for me, he brought me an umbrella one time at work when it was pouring, he opened my car door one day and taped a rose to my steering wheel..."
"Really?"

"Yeah he was so perfect..."

"Did he ever have sex with you ?" Kristina asked

167

"We have sex 5 sometimes 6 times a week.."

"What! That motherfucker wasn't doing that with me, Twice a week if that, that asshole."

"We laid in my bathtub for three hours last week, we got out of the tub because his back was hurting" said Inez

"That bastard told me he hurt his back in the gym, I stood up 3 hours massaging his fucking back" chimed Kristina

"Do you know that he covered my daughters bed in rose petals last month and when my daughter was sick he bought her 100 roses?" instigated Inez' mother

Kristina nodded her head in disbelief as a tear ran down her cheek.

"Those are beautiful earings" said Inez

"Thank you, that motherfucker bought me these, he bought me my car, he bought me a lot of things."

"Well you know he wants to have a baby with my daughter right?" Instigated Inez' mom again

"Baby!? We're trying to have a baby right now!" yelled Kristina

They tried to topple each others lies to make themselves feel like they were the one. Then the baby lies started. They took the baby thing and didn't know that each one of them had the same thing in mind.

"Does he wear a condom with you?" asked Inez

"We're trying to have a baby, why would he?"

"and you?"

Torn

"He comes inside of me all the time"

As tuff as they were trying to be with each other, they ended up breaking each of themselves down. Tears ran down both there faces. Inez sniffled grabbed her cell phone and dialed Tony's number.
"Hello"

"Tony can you please come over I need to talk to you"

"Inez what's wrong, why do you sound like that, are you ok?"

"Just come please, I need you."

"What's wrong honey?"

"Tony please."

"ok, gimme an hour" He hung up.

They toasted their drinks and waited.

****

Monday Afternoon

Ray headed to the airport with Frankie. He called George.

"Hello?"

"George it's me Ray."

"Ray what's up?"

"Hey I'm on my way to the airport I'm going to Miami to pick up that money. I'm buying your ticket at the counter. It'll all be paid for. It will be for tonight at 8:30pm and I'll meet you at the Carlton Hotel at midnight alright?"

169

"Alright bro, hey I'll probably bring my cousin with me alright?"

"Ok but I'm only covering you"

"Na don't worry about it, I got him."

"OK, see you tonight."

****

Tony started to wrap things up at the office when Maddy, his secretary chimed in

"Tony you have Gina on line 1"

"Hello?"

"Hi Tony?" She said sniffling

"What's wrong Gina, what's the matter?"

Gina started to cry.

"I miss Ray, Tony, I love my husband. I want to make everything up to him." she said crying

"Oh boy" Tony said under his breath

"I'm gonna tell him everything Tony."

"No Gina, don't tell him anything, what are you crazy?"

"but wouldn't that be the best way, being honest about everything?"

Tony could not believe his ears.

"You should've thought about being honest before you did what you did, babe, now is not the time to be a saint honey."

"but why, Tony?"

"Look Gina you tell Ray about anything that you did and..."
"He already has pictures." she interrupted

"Yeah but he doesn't have pictures of George, and if he finds out it's George it's not going to be nice for George, it's not gonna be nice for you and it's certainly not going to be nice for me because I brought him into your home."

"I don't know Tony..."

"Gina don't you dare slip up like that"

"Look Tony it's my decision, he's my husband and if I tell him not to do anything to anybody he won't I know him."

"Gina please," Tony pleaded.

"Don't worry Tony your name won't come up" click she hung up

"Fuck!!" Tony yelled.

"Are you o.k.?" Maddy asked

"Oh Maddy Maddy, yeah I'm alright, Hey get me George on the line please, Quickly. I need to warn him, this might be a bad situation."

"Ok, I'll try him now."

She tried and tried for a ½ hour but kept getting his voice mail.

"Tony, I tried but nothing"

"Thanks Maddy I'll try him in a bit"

Tony grabbed his briefcase and headed out the door toward Inez' house.

He put the white beast in overdrive and hurried over. He pulled up to the house and parked the car. He entered the 3 family brick home, took the flight of stairs up and knocked on the door.

Knock knock knock

The door opened. He walked in and looked to the left, down the long corridor that lead to the living room, kitchen, bathroom and the two bedrooms. It was quiet, a little too quiet. He had been here before on some of the quietest days and never had it been this quiet. He stood there, staring down the corridor to his left, waiting for some sort of justification as to why it was so quiet. Standing there, he slowly threw his right hand behind him—catching the door and slowly shutting it. He broke his stare away from the corridor and looked to his right, where the third bedroom door was wide open. He entered the bedroom.

"Close the door" she said.

He obediently closed the door and looked at her, staying close to the door. It was plain to see that something was wrong. It just wasn't the norm. She didn't look happy to see him. She wasn't bubbling over with excitement like she usually was.

"What"? he asked .

She stood quiet, almost as if she was making a mental count. After at least a minute, she came to life and asked, *"Tony, do you love me"?*

"Baby, of course I love you, you know that, why on earth would even-"

Without warning the door swung open and a second woman entered the room.

"How the fuck could you do this to me Tony!? Why the fuck Tony? Why? Haven't I been good to you?!

Tears fell from the second woman's eyes and stained her beautiful pale cheeks with dark eyeliner. Tony glanced to his left and saw the first woman, just sitting there - the mastermind of this whole fiasco, eyes swelled, tears trickling down her face and staining her rose colored cheeks with mascara. His heart was crushed.

"Tony, how could you do this to me? How can you betray my love like that? I work all fucking day hard Tony—10 and 12 hours a day, and this is what you do while I'm at work?!" yelled the first woman.

She was clearly crying her heart out. Standing by the door, were five other women - sisters and mothers of the two girls involved. These were the women to whom he had promised never to hurt either of the girls. They stood there expecting an explanation that he could not give. From the right came screams and tears, from the left came silence and tears, and in his heart arose a bone-crushing pain for fear of losing either one of these beautiful women. He would never be able to express to them how much he loved them both.

Just watching their agony made him wish he were dying in a burning car, rather than seeing them suffer this way. He had promised to make them happy. At the moment, however, he just stood there in silence, his heart hammering so loud, he could've sworn it was audible. It hurt so much, he couldn't even speak.

"What are you going to do now, huh? Is it going to be me or her? Choose now Tony, now!"

He looked at the second girl standing near the door, then to the girl sitting on the bed, just sobbing her little broken heart out. Based on past experiences, this should have been an easy choice to make, right? All he had to do was look at them, weigh the options, see which one he loved more, and choose. Tony, however, was born without the chromosome that would allow him to be cold and unsympathetic. He knew that choosing one would make the other one hurt even more, and yes, he tried to weigh the options and compare them but they were both equal to him. ways, both loving, great families, incredible human beings, and amazing in bed. Again

173

the screams came from the door.

"Do you love her Tony? Tell me now!"

Tony asked himself, "Why is it that when these situations present themselves, the only question that seem to be of any importance to them is *"Do you love her?" I don't get it."*

He felt as if he was in the middle of a tornado.

At the moment, he decided that the best thing for him to do was to put his arms around his back, grab his wrist tightly to avoid any physical reactions, and clench his teeth in preparation for the slap that he knew would eventually come. He lowered his head in shame and thought to himself, *"My God, I have to make a choice right here and now. Please help me to do this right."*

He waited, and waited, but nothing came. Perhaps God wanted him to stew in his own juices for awhile. Tony looked to his left, straight into those beautiful brown eyes that he loved so much, and then to his right, straight into those gorgeous moist eyes that he adored so immensely. He definitely couldn't choose. He looked past the one on his right, only to discover that the front door to the house was slightly open.

"I don't believe you Tony!"

The second girl threw her hands up in the air, and as she turned, she left enough room for him to beeline right past her and through the door. He ran downstairs, jumped into his car, and pulled out of there like a bat out of hell.

They both stared at each other with tears in their eyes.

"Well well ladies there's no point in crying over spilled milk, come lets drink to that slick scumbag son of a bitch Tony." said Inez' mother as she carried drinks on a serving tray.

Torn

"C'mon lift your glasses, here's to his dick falling off" They all raise their arms and toasted.

He fumbled with his phone and called his sister, someone he trusted and could count on with anything. He couldn't dial the number. He was shaking from all the adrenaline that was pumping in his body. He finally got it right.

"Hello Barbie?"

"yeah"

"Yo Barbie these two fucking girls got together and busted me!"

"What? What 2 chicks?"

"Kristina and Inez"

"Who's Inez, who's Kristina?"

"Oh my god, the two chicks I've been telling you about."

"Damn tone, Where you at?"

"I'm on my way to JP's, meet me there"

"alright I'll pass by after work."

"aight bye"

He dialed Chris Dream boy.

"Chris?"

"Yo tone what's up my brother?"

"oh man, I need to talk to you bro."

"What happened?"

"Mann Chris I got busted."

"Busted?"

"Yeah bro, these 2 girls set me up"

"What do you mean, the chick who you met at the club?"

"Yeah, she was one of them the other one was from JP's."

"Oh shit the waitress that's right" he remembered

" I'm going to JP's meet me there"

"Ok, I'll meet you there in 20 minutes"

Tony pulled into the JP's parking lot and parked. He walked through the doors and was greeted by the owner.

"There he is, what's up Tony? You look rough are you ok?"

"hey John, yeah I'm alright just having a rough day"

John motioned over one of the beautiful twins and pointed at Tony.

"Listen twin, he gets everything on the house, Take him to the K room he's expecting people."

"How many are coming Tony?" asked John

"4 John"

"You got it Tony, you want the usual?"

"Yeah just send it all back there, please."

Fifteen minutes later the 6'1" 230 lb monstrosity Chris Dream boy walked through the doors sporting a 2000 watt smile.

"Whoa big guy how ya doing ?" asked John

"Hey mister John how are you? Is our friend here?"

"Yeah he's in the back, what do you want me to send ya?"

"Vodka martini for me and Mojito for our buddy."

"OK"

Big Chris made his way to the back where upon his arrival he saw Tony talking to the twin. Her smile was electric. She had a striking resemblance to a young Sharon Stone.

"Hey tone? What's up buddy?"

"Hey Chris what's up man, this is Jessie."

"Pleasure to meet you Jessie, wow you're fast, you were just at the front making drinks."

She smiled, *"that was probably my sister you saw."*

"Oh shit, Twins?"

She smiled *"Yeah"*

"Tone what do you think, me and you her and her sister?" Chris started laughing

"Na man I don't think we're there types bro, anyway I've got a situation."

"Ok, guys I'll be back" she excused herself and leaves.

Five minutes later Tony's sister walked toward the back area with her girlfriend Venus.

"Hey, Sis!?"

"What's up bro, Hi Chris this is my girlfriend Venus" she says

"So Tone, start from the beginning, I ordered all the food and drinks and it's Gonna keep flowing."

****

Rays plane landed in Miami. 7:30pm he turned on his cell phone. The screen read and beeped 1 missed call. Ray punched in his code and put the phone to his ear.

"One missed call, please press 5 to retrieve your message." said the recording.

Ray pressed 5 and waited.

"Honey? Hi I just wanted to say that I was sorry for what I did to you. Please Ray if you could ever forgive me, I swear I'd never look at another man as long as I live. Look I know I was wrong, but It takes two and If your friend was a little more respectful this would've never happened."

Ray jolted up and sat in his chair, he covered one ear with his hand to be sure he heard everything clear. He listened.

"Yeah I came on to him but he responded Ray, he responded and treated me like you never did. He listened to me and gave a shit about a lot of the things that you didn't. He wanted me for him by himself not to share me with his friends. Those things made me feel like you never did. Anyway I hope you find it in your heart to give me one more chance, bye. Oh by the way since I'm now being honest about everything, I think you should know your friend was George."

Ray stood up in a rage and banged his head on the overhead storage compartment.

"Fuck! Frankie that fucker is the one that was fucking my wife."

"who?!"

"George, the son of a bitch who's ticket I bought and is meeting us tonight."

"The one you're gonna give the money to?"

"Yeah, well fuck that! You fucked my wife behind my back you just fucked yourself!"

The aircraft speakers came alive.

"Please exit the aircraft to your left, you can pick up your belongings on level A. Thank you for flying Jet Blue."

They exited the aircraft. The humidity hit them like a brick wall.

"Damn it's hot in here." said Frankie

"I need a pay phone now" Ray rushed to a payphone and dialed.

"Fuck Fuck Fuck, pick up motherfucker!" Ray was fuming.

"This is Tony please leave a message"

"Tony! That Motherfucker George, that son of a bitch, I'll kill that cocksucker spic motherfucker, where are you? Call me back!".

****

3 hours later Tony, Chris, Venus and Barbie were still drinking and eating.

"What time is it?" Tony asked

Chris looked at his wrist *"11:30"*

Tony looked at his phone wondering why hasn't it rang in over 3 hours. The screen read

"no signal"

"Hey I'm gonna step[outside where I can get reception, I need to check my messages, OK?"

They all acknowledged. Tony stepped out and the phone came to life with message reminders. Tony dialed in to check his messages.

"2 missed calls"

Tony punched in his pass code.

"Hey tone what's up it's me George, I'm flying out to meet Ray in Miami, my flight was a little delayed but I'm boarding now, I'll call you when I get there. My battery is dying so I'll need time to charge it. Bye."

"second message"

"Tony! That Motherfucker George, that son of a bitch, I'll kill that cocksucker spic motherfucker, where are you? He was the one in the fucking pictures. Call me back!".

Tony's eyes flared open. He quickly hung up and tried to call George but got only his voice mail, after 10 attempt he left a message.

"George, He knows bro, please don't go meet Ray, he knows it was you with Gina. Call me back now!"

Tony ran inside and explained the situation, they asked for the check, John comped the whole thing, $345.00. They left the waitress a $200 tip and left.

****

George arrived in Miami as he made his way out of the aircraft he turned on his phone.

"Beep, low batt" the phone flashed then went dead.

"Fuck, I need a charger for this phone now" said George

"You don't have an extra battery?" his cousin chino asked

"no man, not on me"

They stopped at avis, rented a car and drove off. They jumped on the I95 and headed toward South Beach.

****

It was past midnight in the parking lot of the Carlton Hotel and Ray was leaning on the hood of his Lexus GS 400, both elbows on the hood, bent at the waist. His partner, Frankie, was sitting in the passenger's seat with a nine millimeter pistol on his lap. Frankie, sticking his head out the window, called out to Ray.

"Yo, what time is he supposed to be here?"

"I don't know—midnight maybe?" said Ray.

"Well you know it's 12:30 right?

"Relax bro, he'll be here alright? Damn."

A figure crept up behind the car stealthily. It then stood up and opened its arms.

"Yo Ray!" shouted the figure.

Ray moved away from the hood and looked towards the back of the car, where the voice had originated.

"Hey, what's up bro? I've been waiting since midnight, what happened?"

"Oh, you know —just got caught up at the airport. You know, since 9-11 all the security has been off the hook. Ray, this is my brother-in-law Chino."

"What's up Chino." said Ray.

Chino nodded, confirming his identity.

"Let me get that stuff for you bro." said Ray, his attention back on his friend.

Ray walked towards the back of the car and leaned in through the open door, pulling out "that" bag—the one that guy had come for. A single drop of sweat slid down Ray's face. He knew it wouldn't go down that easy. Without warning, Ray dug into his pocket and pulled out a chrome 9 millimeter. In a stroke of bad luck, the 9 millimeter got stuck in Ray's oversized jersey, giving the guy enough time to react and wrench the pistol out of his hand. At the same time, Chino had managed to grab Frankie's neck into a headlock, in an attempt to wrestle the gun out off of him. With the butt of Ray's own gun, the guy smacked the right side of Ray's head. The blow rocked Ray badly, and brought him to his knees. At that moment, Chino managed to wrestle the 9 millimeter off of Frankie, turning his own gun against Frankie's temple. Right before Ray could regain his composure, he was sent crashing to the floor with another blow against his head. A wide split appeared on the left side of his forehead.

The guys, still unnamed, called out to Chino.

"Chino are you alright?"

Torn

"Yeah man, you?"

"Yeah man. I'm good. I can't believe this motherfucker man! He was going to kill me, why?" he shouted.

He turned around in a frenzy and started screaming.

"You piece of shit! You fuckin' cocksucker? Why? Why you fuck?"

Ray in silence offered no response.

"Give me the key to the motherfuckin' room, now! You fuckin' scumbag!"

Ray gave him the bloodied key.

"Now get up and get in the fuckin' room you worm!"

He grabbed Ray by the back of his jersey and dragged him towards the door of the room, while simultaneously "pistol whipping" him on the back of his head. Ray opened the door and Chino forced Frankie inside.

"Take off your clothes!" Chino yelled in his Spanish accent.
Frankie stripped completely.

"Now get over there in that corner, and get on your knees!"

Frankie immediately obeyed. However, Ray remained at the foot of the door on his hands and knees.

"Get up!" said the guy.

Ray began to push himself up, but just as he was about to get on his feet the guy took a step back and plunged his foot square across Ray's back, sending him crashing onto the hotel room floor. Frankie stayed in the corner, shaking like a leaf.

"Ray! Get on your knees now!"

Ray lay there in silence without moving. The guy, infuriated, ran up, put the pistol against Ray's cheekbone, and slowly and deliberately said, *"Get on your fuckin' knees before I blast your fuckin' ass, motherfucker!"*

Ray complied and finally knelt in front of the guy. The guy put a single finger under Ray's chin and positioned his face so that he could look directly into Ray's eyes.

"Ray, bro, you were going to kill me? Over money bro? All of the things we've shared, all the times we've had, and all the money we've made? Yet, you were going to kill me over $30,000 bro?"

Crrraaaack! He delivered yet another blow against Ray's already injured forehead. Infuriated, the guy continued to bashing away at the wound on Ray's head. The more he bashed, the more blood gushed out of the wound. Ray started to make a slight swerving movement, as if he was on the verge of passing out. In an effort to avoid any more pain Ray swung his arm across the gun as it was coming down for another blow.

"BAM!"

The gun went off and Ray crumbled over like a bag of rocks. He clutched his chest and looked up at the guy as he stood over him.

"Let me go to the hospital, please!" Ray pleaded.

The guy stood there in silence, shocked over what had just happened. Chino looked over at Frankie kneeling in the corner and yelled at him.

"Don't you fucking move from there!"

"Please., please, bro let me go to the hospital. I won't say anything to anybody. Please bro, I swear on my life bro. Come on you know

my wife bro, and I would never want to put her life in jeopardy. Let me go get this taken care of please!" pleaded Ray.

The guy took three steps back away from Ray and said, *"Ray, you told me you had money, and despite that it's been over seven months that I've been waiting. I never threatened or harassed you for it. As a matter of fact, you called me to come and meet you—that you had my money already. You called me bro. Why would you want to kill me Ray?*

The silence was deafening.

"I'm leaving Ray. When I leave, your friend can take you to the hospital.

They both jumped into the rental, breathing hard and taking in everything that just happened. The silence was deafening. The drove for an hour before chino spoke.

"Bro what just happened?"

"That motherfucker, didn't you see, he wanted to kill me over fucking money, that fucker!"

"Cono, man what are we gonna do George?"

"We need to get back to NY. First flight out" He stopped the car abruptly and got out to use the payphone. He started to retrieve his messages.

"Beep"

"George, He knows bro, please don't go meet Ray, he knows it was you with Gina. Call me back now!"

"Beep"

George knew he fucked up. He clutched the phone to his chest and put his head down.

He gathered himself and called the airport for morning reservations. Then he dialed Tony.

"Hello?" Tony answered

"Hey buddy what's up?"

"Holy shit George, Listen don't meet with ray, he knows! He knows about you and Gina."

"No No I went to meet him and he never showed up, I'll be back in NY in a couple of days."

"OK, see you when you get here."

"Bye"

****

"Doctor he's going into cardiac arrest"

The nurses dragged the defibrillator toward the body.

"Ready, clear!"

The paddle jolted the lifeless body off of the gurney. The solid beep continued.

"He's gone, hang it up. Time of death 3:58am. Call the wife."

****

Thursday morning

The buzzer rang

Torn

"who's there?"

"George" Tony opened the door and hugged him.

"Damn bro, you said you were coming back three days ago, what the hell happened? Man the shit that's happened to me lately has been fucking unbelievable."

"I was tying up loose ends ya know"

"What are all these bags?"

"Oh, I wanted to ask you if it was alright that I crash here for a couple of weeks?"

"Of course bro, you're my brother man, is everything ok?"

"Yeah yeah man everything's good"

"Well here, this is a copy of my keys, come and go as you please I'll be at my office, here are my office numbers. I'll see you tonight at about 4pm. We'll go for drinks and I'll tell you everything that's happened."

"Oh by the way Tone do me a favor, go to my house, the one you sold me and get a for sale sign up there bro, I think I'm gonna dump it."

"Yo, George are you sure everything's alright man?" Tony asked

"C'mon tone I know what I'm doing, trust me."

"Ok, give me the keys"

George tossed him the keys. Tony left and headed towards Georges house. He arrived and pulled 2 for sale signs from his trunk. He went inside and placed the signs on the window. He left the house and was confronted by 4 men.

"How you doing sir, this house for sale?" said the one of the men *"yes, yes it is. Are you interested?"*

"Maybe, do you have a card?"

"yes, here you go." Tony handed them each a card.

"Please feel free to call me at anytime, I'll make an appointment for anyone of you to take a look inside."

"ok," They shook Tony's hand and left.

Tony headed to the office. He started thinking how the hell did those guys realize the house was for sale so fast. Then he dismissed the thought. He arrived, settled in and started to finish up contracts for 2 properties. He pressed the intercom button on his desk.

"Maddy?"

"Yes Tony?"

"Maddy, can you please bring me a diet Pepsi?'

"Sure"

"Thank you sweety"

She brought him the diet Pepsi *"anything else?"*

"No, I'm good maddy thanks."

10 minutes had passed when Tony's intercom rang.

"Tony?"

"Yeah"

"There are 6 gentlemen here to see you"

Torn

"ok, send them in"

The 6 men casually dressed in jeans and sneakers walked in, they looked serious.

Tony recognized 4 of them.

"Hey fellas, Interested in that house?" *They were the four that had approached Tony at George's house*

"No, what we are interested in is knowing where we can find George Selbor."

"I'm sorry guys who did you say you were?"

In what seemed to be a rehearsed action, 2 of them pulled there badges out of there shirts and the other 4 flashed there wallets.

"Miami Dade Police Dept, are you going to tell us where he is or are we gonna have to play hardball with your punk ass?"

Tony grew cold, stiff and clammy.

"I'm sorry, what is this about?"

"We know that you know where we can find George."

In one swift motion they threw 4 photos of George on Tony's glass desk. Tony picked up one of the photos that displayed George and his mother. He stared at the photos knowing that they had the right name.

"What did he do, Officers, if I may ask?"

"He's wanted for homicide"

"Homicide, you must have the wrong guy, he wouldn't hurt a fly fellas. I know this guy."

189

"Well you just let us do our job and we'll determine if he would hurt a fly or not."

Tony grabbed the photos again and stared intensely, then looked up.

"Sorry fellas, can't help ya"

"Listen here you motherfucker we know you know where he's at, so you either tell us where we can find him or you're fucking going down with him, you hear me you dumb fuck!" The detectives knew he was lying, but Tony was not about to hand George over just like that. The other officer interjected.

"Listen you're a smart guy, look around you all this is yours, do you really want to risk losing it all over a drug king ping?"

"Drug King Ping?" Asked Tony surprisingly

"Yeah drug fucking king ping, you fucking asshole, and so help me god you're going down with him" Yelled the Florida detective.

Tony stared at the Florida cop as intensely as he was giving it. The N.Y. Fugitive officer then stood up and passed Tony a business card.

"Here you go, please, this is a fugitive and a wanted man. If you see him please call us."

"Ok, no problem officer."

They all backed away from the door and exited the building. Tony stood frozen, staring at the business cards. They were gone.

"This fucking guy" he thought to himself. Tony started putting together thoughts and pieces that would solidify their claims about George being a Drug King Ping.

His meeting with Ray, his throwing money around like it was water, his traveling habits. He stared at the wall clock as it passed 4, 5, 6, 7,

8 PM. He got up, locked his door and climbed the flight that led to the exit. A glass door stood between Tony and the street. He looked through the glass and stared at the parked cars on the street.

"No one sitting in any parked cars"

He looked for anything out of the ordinary, everything seemed normal. He pushed the glass door open and headed toward his car. He took off but instead of taking a left turn to go home he took a right turn, so did plenty of cars after him. He accelerated the pedal, while he looked through his rear view mirror.

"7 sets of headlights, fuck! Who's who!"
As he drove he contemplated his next move, a sudden right turn.

"GO" He whipped the steering wheel to the right and immediately looked at the rear view.

"6 sets fuck!"

He stared at his mirror and 2 sets dropped off, 4 cars still coming. Tony made 3 more random turns and 2 cars remained. Then he thought Pennyfield Ave, a street about 2 miles long. If they were following him he'd be sure to know about it then. The 2 mile stretch had no street lamps so the only light that were seen were headlights. He turned onto Harding Ave still 2 sets, Pennyfield is coming in 5, 4, 3, 2, 1 block and he turned onto Pennyfield Ave. He quickly looked at the mirror and watched as the cars kept going.

They never turned. Tony drove the whole 2 miles till the end in which you have to make a U- turn. He made the turn and parked, shutting off the car and positioned in the opposite direction. No cars came through for 2 whole hours.

Tony fired up the engine and headed home in a fury.

Tony entered the elevator and pressed the button furiously. The doors opened, he walked out and stood in front of his apartment door, He began pounding his door with his fist forgetting that he had his house keys on him.

"Bang bang bang, George open the fucking door!"

The sound of clicking locks and peephole openings were heard. The locks unlatched and the door opened.

"Yo, what the fuck did you do?" Tony yelled as he barged in.

"Nothing bro…"

"There were 6 fucking cops in my office earlier today, looking to take you down bro.

They said you killed somebody and that you were a drug king ping, Talk to me bro? what the fuck is going on?"

George scrambled to get his stuff, grabbed his bags and ran out of the apartment. In a rage Tony intercepted George at the door and threw him against the wall.

"Is it true bro"

George looked at Tony knowing he could no longer lie.

"Yes but it was an accident Tony."

Tony knew he couldn't let George get jammed up.

"Take the second door out the building that leads toward the back, I'll go out the front in case they followed me they'll continue to follow me and you can go"

"Ok Tone, hey do me a favor, look after my son, he's gonna need a dad and I don't trust anyone."

"Ok bro"

Just like that George was gone.

****

1 month later

Tony sat in his office replaying the messages that both Kristina and Inez had left over a month ago. They both still wanted to be with Tony and were both willing to forgive him but neither wanted to share him. It really didn't matter what they wanted because Tony wanted them both and that was what he intended to do. His cell phone rang.

"Hello?"

"Tone?"

"Who's this?"

"Me nigga George"

"Holy shit, bro where are you!?"

"Very far and it's better that you don't know"

"George what really happened man?"

"Tony Ray tried to kill me that night in Florida, over money. So I took his gun and started beating him on the head with it then he tried to block one of the blows and the gun accidentally went off and hit him in the shoulder, he died in the hospital Tony."

"Bro they said you were a drug king ping is that true?"

"Na, I'm no king ping Tony, look I'm sorry I got you involved, I should've been straight up with you"

"You think?" Tony said sarcastically

"Hey George I've been spending a lot of time with your son, I'm going to treat him as if he were my own."

"Thank you tone, listen tone can you do me a favor bro?"

"What is it?"

"I'm low on cash..."

"I don't have any cash ..."

"Let me finish, I need you to call this guy name Harry, he owes me $30,000 tell him to give it to you and I'll call you to let you know where you can leave it. That's it"

"Ok, what's the number?"

"347-883-9917- call me at this number when you're done, 809-774-8331."

"OK, hey George, will I ever see you again?"

"Yeah after a couple of years when things cool down, I'll be back"

"OK bro take good care."

****

Through the next 30 days Tony saw Kristina off and on. They fought 4 of the 7 days in the week. When they were off Tony was on with Inez but he was never on with both.

September 28th

Tony was at Inez's house running coaxial cable for Inez's DSL line when his phone rang.

"Hello?"

"Hello can I speak to Tony?"

"Speaking"

"This is Harry, I have what you requested for George."

"Where do you want to meet?" asked Tony

"Lets meet at Bruckner Plaza by the McDonalds', I have a silver Mercedes"

"OK, I've got a white car, 10 minutes"

Tony got up off his knees and yelled towards the bedroom.

"Babe, I'll be back in a half hour!"

"OK, baby!" she shouted back Tony drove by the area once and didn't see anything or anyone there. He went around and drove by again, this time the grey Benz was there. Tony pulled into the lot and parked head on facing the Mercedes. The guy waved him over. Tony got out, opened the Mercedes' passenger door and got in. He was instantly recognized by Harry, a dark skinned potbellied Dominican.

"Oh shit, you're a stripper right?"

"yeah, yeah how'd you know?"

"You've danced for my sister and I had you in my clubs many times China Club, Exit and The Cheetah Club."

"oh alright" Tony did not recall.

They shook hands and Tony looked around.

"Ok I gotta jet, you got the money?"

"Well my man is supposed to drop it off to us in a few minutes but yo where the hell is George?"

"I don't know man."

Tony changed the subject and for the next twenty minutes they spoke about stripping, Real Estate and Clubs.

"Hey Tony listen, I think this guy wants to give George the money directly bro."

"Hey look bro, George asked me to do him a favor to pick up this money for him alright? Now if your friend has a problem with that you fix it with him. I'm here as a favor for my brother, if you really care about him you make sure your friend has no problems about giving me this money."

"But Tone you said you didn't know where he was, what if you take the money and run?"

"Look man, I'm sorry I'm just a little anxious. I speak to George daily, when all those cops were looking for him he was at my house, but I wasn't going to give him up like that."

"Hmm, I see" said Harry.

A green Cherokee jeep pulled in front of the passenger door blaring the high beams temporarily blinding Tony.

"Ok here's my boy with your money"

Tony tried to look through the window at the jeep's windshield to see who was driving, all he saw was black. Then his heart dropped. He saw red and yellow strobe lights turning in circles.

"Fuck!!" He looked to his left and a swarm of undercover cops sped

up to the grey Mercedes, all sporting flashing red strobe lights and flashing headlights.

The passenger door swung open, they grabbed Tony's arm, pulled him out and threw him against the hood of the car. His head laid flat against the hood of the car facing the windsheild. His eyes pierced the windsheild as he looked into Harry's eyes, an X drug dealer turned snitch when he was busted with 25 kilos of cocaine and willingly agreed to set innocent people up in exchange for time off of his sentence.

The big burley Florida detective bent over the hood looked Tony in the eye smiled and said *" I told you I was taking you down"*

****

The Aftermath

Tony ended up signing a 57 month plea agreement, the charge, lying to a federal agent.

Tony knew he was going away and tried to make clean breaks with both Inez and Kristina but both cried and rejected his idea of a breakup.

Inez finally left and accepted the fact that 4 yrs and 9 mos was a little too long to wait for anyone, especially at her young age. Unfortunately Kristina was not that easy. Tony spoke to Kristina's mother and pleaded for her to talk to her daughter and convince her that being with Tony was not a good Idea. Kristina was not buying it. She told her mother that she wanted to marry Tony. Tony was realistic and knew it wasn't going to happen. He saw both women before turning himself in, the tears and denials were everywhere.

Tony told Ethan he was going to school. Ethan saw so much of his dad in Tony that he wants to live with Tony when he comes home. Kristina wrote and visited 3 times. After 2 weeks Inez broke down and wanted to communicate with Tony. She wrote a letter to Tony's sister on how they spent their last days together and on how she loved him and wanted his contact information. She slipped the letter underneath Tony's apartment door thinking his sister lived there but Kristina found it instead. Kristina never visited again and ended up sleeping with one of Tony's closest friends.

He never heard from Inez again. George was never apprehended and remains a fugitive from justice.

While in prison all of the friends Tony thought he had either stole from him, abandoned him or never wrote. Of the strippers big Chris Dream boy, Rob Desire and Nastee Boy all wrote. People who didn't know Tony was incarcerated found out and wrote.

In life many times you are Torn into making decisions that will alter the course of your life forever. It will turn you from the man you were to the man you will become. Tony was Torn between two women and making a decision to lie where if he didn't, the closest thing he had to a brother would've gone to prison for life.

Who knew that a lie would cost him his freedom, his loves and his family.

Tony will be out soon and to those who crossed him he sends a message:

Revenge is Sweet